SLIDING

SLIDING

Jane Foster

Green Dragon Books
Palm Beach, FL
USA

Sliding

A Green Dragon Publishing Group Publication

© 2015 Green Dragon Books

Green Dragon Publishing
2875 S. Ocean Blvd. Suite 200
Palm Beach, FL 33480
http://www.greendragonbooks.com
info@greendragonbooks.com

Printed in the United States of America and the United Kingdom

ISBN (Paperback) 978-1-62386-017-2
ISBN (e-book) 978-1-62386-018-9

Library of Congress Cataloging-in-Publication Data Control #
Author photo © *2013 ASpencerSchwartz@gmail.com*

To my darling children with love

Acknowledgements

I love having this opportunity to thank my family and friends who read, listened and encouraged me along the way during the two years it took to complete SLIDING.

You each made a difference. I thank Kathy Snowden, Augusta Lorber, Giraud Lorber, Peyton Bruns, Tonia Grein, Thomas Flagg, Catharine Hamilton, Marianne Edwards, Billy Wister, Dora Frost, Donna Casey, Dawn Flynn, Martin Lorber, Kate Winsett, Dawn Prosser. Judy Hoffman, Susan Gublemann, Ann Copeland, Polly Norris, Helen Pilkington, Lauren Donovan and Alexis Manice.

And in Paris, I give my special thanks to Bernadette Barbier in whose beautiful apartment I stayed during much of the time writing this book and to Gretel Furner, my teacher, mentor, editor. Also many thanks to Sue Greig, Patricia Gastaud-Gallager, Della Donahue, Cynthia and Christof LeCerf and all of my writing group, especially Anne Yelland and to the staff of La Rotonde who guarded my computer, welcomed and nourished me during the long stays in Paris.

Chapter 1

Hurrying down Madison Avenue, Daphne Hone glimpsed her profile reflected in the window of Georg Jensen's shop, and although she liked the look of her suede boots, she wished she'd worn more sensible shoes. Holding on to the black umbrella, she peered over her shoulder as if the very air were stalking her and picked up her pace. It was eight a.m. on Friday, September 27th, 1985, and Hurricane Gloria was prowling the Atlantic.

Marie had scolded her for going out like this, what with schools closed and Mayor Koch interrupting every program cautioning people to stay home. Daphne told Marie to get the boys baking cookies for the shelters and not to worry about her. She would be home well before noon. Was there enough water? Enough peanut butter?

Usually, Daphne loved the twenty-minute walk to her office in Rockefeller Center. This was the time of day when the city stretched and yawned before getting down to the noisy business of evolving. At this time on any other day, there were dozens of people mutely rushing, heads down, thoughts inward, not making eye contact. She liked being part of this focused, powerful energy surging toward midtown. But today, the few passersby actually looked at her, wondering why she was out on the street when the Mayor wanted everyone in. Hardly a car or taxi in sight. The eerie quietness unsettled her. She wished she'd taken a Valium or something before setting out.

The wind picked up as she turned west toward Fifth Avenue. She pulled the umbrella lower, spokes biting her scalp. The purple waterproof jacket with the velvet collar was frivolous in the face of what was predicted, and the black jeans, too sexy. She knew it was crazy ignoring the hurricane warnings, but she could be home within the hour. All she needed was the letter, hand-delivered the afternoon before, a letter from her ex-husband's lawyer, demanding some outrageous sum of money no doubt.

Skirting the massive bronze sculpture of Atlas holding the world on his shoulders, Daphne entered the gleaming lobby. The building superintendent was standing alone at the first bank of elevators. She waved and smiled, the sound of her high-heeled boots echoing in the cavernous emptiness.

"Ms. Hone, the building's officially closed. I can let you up but not for more than an hour. We're going to lock up before ten so we can get home before the subway shuts down."

"I'll only be a few minutes. Thanks, Eddy."

Daphne's body was tense. She pulled at her rain jacket self-consciously as she waited for the elevator doors to open.

Her umbrella dripped on the elevator floor as she stared blankly at the mirror. Pulling a tube of lip-gloss out her pocket, she slapped it on, more out of habit than vanity. She pulled the sides of her fat ponytail out to tighten the red scrunchie, tendrils seeping out on both sides. Reaching the seventh floor, she turned left down the empty hall, jingling keys in her hand.

The sign on the door read: Richard Blake, Gemologist. Flipping on the lights as she entered the silent reception room, Daphne went straight to her office. The envelope was there, front and center, on top of a neat pile of papers. Still standing, she ripped it open, scanning the contents.

"Bastard," she muttered and dialed the lawyer's number, the number she had known by heart since childhood. If anyone were at work that morning it would be Ludlow Fowler.

"Fowler here." She loved his gravely voice, seasoned by decades of cigar smoke.

"Uncle Ludlow, I had a letter from Kenny's lawyer."

"What's up?"

"Well, the good news is that he's agreed to the name change. The bad news is he's demanding $100,000 for it." Daphne's blonde and handsome ex-husband had done very well in getting their loft as well as alimony in the divorce, but he wanted more and now saw a way to get it.

Ludlow let out a long sigh. "That son of a bitch. Sorry, Daphne, but you really picked a rotter."

"I know. And what a sum."

"He knows you can afford it, but this is preposterous. I'll see what I can do."

"Thanks, Uncle Ludlow. Wish I'd listened to you in the first place."

"Have you told the boys yet?"

"No. Not yet."

"We promised your mother…. I know you'll handle it well."

"I've talked to the school psychologist who gave me some good suggestions. Apparently, this is not the first time something like this has happened at the Wilson School."

"Nor the last, I'd be willing to bet."

"I'd better be getting home now," Daphne said.

"Don't tell me you're out."

"I only came to get the letter. Kenny called last night demanding a response, and I hadn't read it yet. I left early yesterday to pick up the boys. Anyway, I see you're in *your* office."

"I was just leaving when you called. Are you there alone? Is Richard there?"

"He's in Geneva for the Sotheby's sale."

"I can pick you up in fifteen minutes. I insist upon taking you home. Go stand by Atlas. I'm on my way."

By the time Daphne reached Fifth Avenue, the wind was stronger with heavy rain shafting down. She felt a cold shiver scale her spine. As a destructive force, Hurricane Gloria had nothing on her ex-husband, Kenny. Was the worst of that tempest over now? She wondered.

The dark blue Lincoln pulled up to the curb, and Daphne hopped quickly into the back seat so the chauffeur, Fred, would not get wet. He was getting older, almost as old as her Godfather, and she knew his knees were stiff. "Good morning, Uncle Ludlow, Fred. Neither of you look concerned about Gloria, I see."

"We are, though. As soon as we've dropped you off and made sure you've battened down the hatches, we'll head home." Ludlow moved over, avoiding the soaking umbrella.

It was typical of Ludlow to worry about her. He'd known her since the day she was born. After his wife's death, he'd never remarried, and Daphne was like a daughter to him.

"I wish you two would spend the storm with us, Uncle Ludlow. We have plenty of room." The plea in her voice surprised her.

"I'm sorry, darling. I have to get back to those sissy dogs of mine. They skulk under the bed at the first peal of thunder. This is their first hurricane, so heaven knows what they'll do. Fred's going to stay with me for the weekend and help reassure them. Right, Fred?"

"But what about us? Don't we need reassuring, too?" Daphne stretched her shoulders slightly, trying to ease the tension.

"You've got Marie there, and what about Lionel? Can't he stay?"

"I hate to ask Lionel. He lives with his mother in Queens. But I guess I could ask him to go pick her up, and we could all hunker down together at my place."

"Now, there's a sensible idea."

The car slowed to a halt in front of an impressive limestone townhouse on the north side of 70th Street between Park and Lexington. It had been in the Hone family since the 1920s when her grandfather built it with profits from his railroad speculation. Fred got out with a golf umbrella and saw Daphne and Ludlow to the door.

"I'll be ready to go in fifteen minutes, Fred. See if William Poll is open, and if they are, get six containers of watercress dip and charge it, please," Ludlow said.

"Yes, sir."

"And get some of those toast chips and frozen soup, too."

"Right you are, Mr. F. Can I get something for you, Miss Daphne?"

"We're all set. Thanks, Fred." Daphne loved the soft Irish lilt in his voice.

"Daphne, there's something I'd like to discuss with you. Nothing serious - don't look so worried." Ludlow took her elbow and steered her through the door.

"Let's go up to the library. We won't be disturbed there." Before they walked up the curving marble staircase to the main floor of the townhouse, Daphne peeped into the kitchen where her two sons were, elbow deep in cookie dough. Without stopping to say hello, she continued upstairs with Ludlow.

The walls of the library were lacquered the color of eggplant and a sisal rug covered most of the floor. Daphne went straight for her customary spot on the sky blue sofa and sat fidgeting with the fringe on a cushion. Ludlow followed to his favorite armchair near the window and began.

"I just found out Johnny's coming for the annual meeting in October. He called yesterday and said he'd be coming alone."

"Would you like a glass of sherry, Uncle Ludlow?"

Raising his bushy eyebrows, he replied, "Good grief, Daphne. It's only nine o'clock in the morning."

'I've been up so long it seems like lunchtime to me. What were you saying about Johnny?" Daphne's half-brother lived with his fashion-model wife and their daughter in London.

"I was just saying he's coming alone, and that suits me. I find Amelia heavy going. All that 'personality' smothering everyone in the room."

"I know. I think she acts like an idiot to atone for being so tall and thin." Absentmindedly, Daphne pulled out the scrunchie letting her chestnut hair cascade over her shoulders.

"Expensive, too," Ludlow continued. "Johnny tells me he needs more income now. We'll have to discuss how to restructure the investments in October." Ludlow sighed wearily. "I'm getting too old for this."

"Don't worry. I'll go along with whatever he wants to do, but I know he'll always resent me no matter what."

"Johnny's not a bad sort, Daphne. Think of it from his point of view. He was your father's only heir until he was twenty; then you came along and changed everything. He's never said an unkind word about you."

"I know. I know. And, I like him well enough, but now he probably blames me for what happened to Louisa. But I've always adored her, and if you think about it, she's more my age than Johnny is. And my only niece."

"By the way, how *is* Louisa?"

"Really well. I just talked to her yesterday. She moved out of the house and is living with three roommates in a mews house in Knightsbridge. Going to Central St. Martin's studying the fashion industry. She wants to be a designer."

"Well, I'm glad to hear she's doing well after that awful business with Kenny." He got up and held his arms out to Daphne. "Come give an old man a hug. I have to get going before the going gets impossible."

"Call me when you get home."

"Don't be a mother hen. I'll call you tomorrow."

Spotting Ludlow at the front door, Fred hurried up the short path with an umbrella. There was only a slight drizzle now, and the wind had died down. Daphne could hear the birds chattering, settling themselves in the trees. The quiet before the storm, she thought. It won't be long now. Standing in the doorway, Daphne waved as the car headed east toward Long Island.

In the kitchen the boys, dusty with powdered sugar, were just taking the last batch of cookies out of the oven. As Daphne watched her heart swelled with tenderness. "When you guys finish, come up to my room, and we'll watch TV. Marie, do you know where Lionel is?"

"He just went over to Gristede's for a few things. Hope he got there before they close. You know Lionel. He wants everything just right, rain or shine."

"Yes, always prepared for anything and everything. Just as soon as he gets back, tell him to call his mother and ask her to pack their clothes and come spend a day or two here with us. I'll feel safer if we are all together."

"Speak of the devil, and he appears." Marie gave Lionel a broad smile and took one of the grocery bags from him.

"Oh, Lionel, we were just talking about you. I know you Jamaicans are world experts on hurricanes, and I want you to go get your mother and have her join us here, if that is okay with you two."

"Thank you, Mrs. Hone. I'll call her right now. My aunt is staying with us. Would it be all right to bring her, too?"

"Of course! Go get the station wagon and pick them up right away. It's nine-thirty now. You have time, but hurry. And be sure we have plenty of flashlights and batteries."

"We're all set, Mrs. Hone. And I can be back here with my mother and aunt by eleven, eleven fifteen." Daphne knew she could count on Lionel.

By noon, everyone in the Hone house was settled. The boys were on Daphne's bed watching cartoons, and Marie was seasoning a huge pot of vegetable soup, biscuits in the oven.

As predicted, Gloria made landfall on Long Island at two that afternoon. Wind screamed through the empty streets of Manhattan. Lightening lashed the sky. A branch from the linden tree outside Daphne's bedroom window snapped and smashed the glass shattering it behind the duct tape that Lionel had put up the day before and darkness claimed the rest of the day.

Gloria thundered on, and Daphne distracted the boys by reading *Twenty Thousand Leagues Under the Sea* until they fell into a fitful sleep. Maggie, her best friend since third grade, called from Chicago. Daphne didn't want to wake the boys and whispered she would call back when she could. By six the whole household gathered in the family room for the evening news, watching in horror as the reporters showed the devastation happening around them on Long Island and New Jersey.

"Kids, it's a good thing you baked all those cookies today. I'll be sure to get them to the shelters tomorrow."

"Mom, is it okay if Joe and I stay with you until the hurricane is over?" Henry asked.

"Of course. Go get your Lego bricks so you'll have something to do."

They sat in front of the television for hours, as if by keeping the vigil some of the wreckage would right itself. Hurricane force winds howled at the trees, blew them into buildings and across roads, ripped the roofs off of houses, schools and police stations. Over half a million New Yorkers were without power. They said it was a blessing that landfall was at low tide. Even so, reporters called it the 'storm of the century'.

Finally, around midnight, Lionel picked up five-year-old Joe and carried him up to bed, as his mother steered his sleepy older brother to the adjoining room. Dazed, the adults said goodnight and parted, each to their own beds.

Late though it was, after Daphne had put on her pajamas, she went back downstairs and poured herself a large glass of Chardonnay. Despite being safe and dry, the deafening thunder had worked on her nerves, and the wine tasted particularly good that night. The first sip brought a flood of relief to her tensed muscles. Turning the TV back on and lowering the sound, she kicked off her slippers, curled up on the sofa and pulled the phone toward her. Maggie answered on the first ring.

Chapter 2

The next morning Daphne let the boys have breakfast on her bed. "Have you guys ever heard about a family name dying out?" she asked casually.

"You mean like Tyrannosaurus Rex?" Eight-year-old Henry knew all about that.

"Sort of. You know Uncle Johnny has Louisa, but she'll get married and take her husband's name. Remember, after Daddy and I were divorced, I went back to my maiden name, the one I had when I was a little girl? People change their names for lots of different reasons."

"Sure, Mom. We know." Henry looked longingly at the blank TV screen.

"I was thinking, what if you guys changed your last name to Hone? I talked to Daddy, and he agrees it would be sad if there were no more Hones. Daddy has three brothers so there'll be lots of Langs."

"I'm already a Hone," said Joe, standing on the bed pointing at himself. "Joseph Hone Lang. That's me."

"Well, you can be Joseph Lang Hone. How about that?"

"Fine with me." Joe jumped down off the bed.

"Fine with me, too, Mom. Can we watch cartoons now?" Henry was anxious to get to the Smurfs.

"Sure. Go ahead."

The TV drowned out Daphne's sigh of relief. Going down to the library, she tried to call Ludlow, but there was no phone service on Long Island. Just as she was leaving the room, the phone rang. It was her half-brother, Johnny, calling from London. Johnny didn't call often. After all, he was twenty years older, and they had very little in common other than sharing a father and both loving Louisa.

"Daphne! How'd you survive the hurricane? It was all over the news here, and I've been worried about you."

"You're so nice to call. We're fine. We didn't even loose power, but I can't get in touch with Uncle Ludlow. Things are bad on Long Island."

"I know. I couldn't get through to him, either, but he's a tough old bird. I'm sure he's fine."

"You're right, and he has Fred with him."

"Listen. I know you must be busy, but a strange thing happened. I had a phone call yesterday from a woman in Thomasville, Georgia, claiming she's our father's daughter. Do you know anything about this?"

Daphne felt hot, cold then hot again in a matter of seconds. She was not sure she could speak. "No." Breathing in as she spoke, she tipped forward and put all her weight on the desk, not trusting her legs. Betrayal, anger and curiosity fought for her attention. "Who is she, this woman?" Her voice sounded far away from her ears.

"I have no idea. What she wants is money. Quite a lot in fact. Ludlow would be the only person in the world to know if there is any truth in all this. It does sort of sound like our father, though, and since you're there in the right time zone, I'm going to leave it to you to get in touch with Ludlow. Have him call me. The woman's name is Ella Smyth. She sounds young on the phone, about Louisa's age, I would guess."

Johnny seemed in a hurry to get off the phone and offered no more information. Standing with the phone still in her hand, Daphne let the information sink in. She didn't think it sounded like her father. What did Johnny mean by that crack? From what they were saying on the news it was clear she could not just drive out to Long Island to see Ludlow - only authorized emergency vehicles were allowed on the roads, and there was no information as to when power would be restored. Ella Smyth. She noted the name on a piece of paper. Could it be true? Could Ludlow be keeping something secret?

Though the Hones lived in New York, Daphne's father, John Hone, had a plantation in Thomasville, Georgia, where he spent as much time as possible during the hunting season. He had been killed in a shooting accident there when Daphne was twelve. After his death, her mother sold the place lock, stock and barrel, and never returned to the area nor mentioned the accident again. In fact, no one ever mentioned the accident. And her mother rarely mentioned her father. Daphne had not thought this was odd at the time. After all, her mother was grieving the loss of her husband and to talk about him must have been painful. Daphne believed this so strongly that she'd always avoided asking about her father. When she wanted to talk about him, she went to Ludlow. But now…

Within fifteen minutes the phone was ringing again. "Daphne, darling, how're things on 70th Street?"

"Uncle Ludlow! Are you okay? Is your power back on?"

"No power. I walked over to the marina. I'm on a friend's ship-to-shore radio. All I want to hear is that all's well in your household."

"Everything was fine until just now. Johnny called from London. What do you know about a woman called Ella Smyth?"

"Nothing. Why?" Did she detect a hesitation in his voice?

"She called Johnny claiming to be our father's daughter. She lives in Thomasville. Or anyway, she was calling from Thomasville."

Daphne's eyes drifted to a silver framed photograph of her mother taken on the plantation when Daphne was a babe in arms. She was smiling, presenting Daphne to the camera. Had her mother been a happy woman? Daphne had always thought so.

"I can't call London until normal phone service has been restored. But don't worry, Daphne. I'll try and find out more. No doubt this is just some scam or other. I'll get in touch with Johnny as soon as I can. Nothing to concern you. By the way, did you talk to the boys about the name change?"

"Yes, and what an anti-climax that was. They couldn't have cared less. All that time I tortured myself with how best to put it, and really, the Smurfs are much more interesting to them."

"I knew it'd be fine. So glad that's behind you. I'll try to give you a call tomorrow."

"Thanks. I was desperate not knowing how to get in touch with you."

Daphne put the phone down. 'Okay. I won't think about Ella Smyth until I find out more', she said to herself, then called the Red Cross to see what she could do to be helpful to the hurricane victims. Daphne knew many of the Red Cross regulars as her mother had started her there as a volunteer as soon as she was old enough to be useful. Daphne appreciated how lucky she was to have so many privileges and was quick to help others. Spending the rest of the day in her 1979 Ford County Squire, shuttling equipment and volunteers from shelter to shelter was her natural response to this emergency.

By the time Daphne got home that evening, it was nearly seven o'clock and the kitchen was full of people. Nicaraguan and Jamaican specialties were simmering on the stove. Seeing the boys were enjoying the camaraderie, Daphne joined them just long enough to pour a large glass of white wine to take to her room. Exhausted, all she wanted was a bath and bed.

Putting her half drunk glass of wine on the edge of the tub, she slipped into the hot, scented water. By eight she was in bed, chatting to Maggie and enjoying the rest of her wine.

"You know, Maggie, your move to Chicago left a big hole in New York City social life. I know you like your big promotion, and I'm so proud of you, but for me, it's like senior year when your parents suddenly moved to Connecticut. I have no life left." Daphne could hear ice tinkling in Maggie's glass and a cigarette being lit.

"There's no social life out here, either. The people are really nice and friendly, but Chicago's a couples' town. I always seem to be the odd man out. I wish you would ask your Uncle Ludlow if he knows any cute young lawyers for us."

"Oh, please. I couldn't bear it."

"You should marry some nice man, Daphne. The boys need a father. The one they have is unfit for the job."

"I won't even tell you the latest about him." Daphne yawned. "Talk to you tomorrow, Maggie."

Tired as she was, Daphne couldn't fall asleep. Speculation about Ella Smyth rattled her, and then, for some reason, images of Kenny and the episode in the loft came unbidden. She rarely thought about that last night, but there it was roaming around her mind, refusing to go away. It had been two years since that horrible night in Soho, where she and the boys were living back when she was still married to Kenny. Daphne had been in Joe's room quieting him from a nightmare when she heard scuffling coming from the guestroom at the back of the loft where her niece Louisa was staying. She heard Kenny cursing. Out of instinct, she grabbed the butcher's knife from the kitchen on her way to see what was happening. While she hesitated in the doorway with the big knife in her hand straining to see into the dark room, Kenny, half-dressed, hair dripping wet, brushed past her and rushed out the front door. Dumbstruck, Daphne followed him and slid the bolt into the steel-framed door.

She managed to get Louisa into the shower and threw away the ripped nightshirt. At three a.m. she called her mother who was at home in the house where Daphne now lived to tell her what had happened and to say they would be coming right over. Then she telephoned London Town Cars, asked for a van to be sent as soon as possible and packed clothes for them all. Forty minutes later she and Louisa carried the sleeping boys to the van, arriving at the Hone townhouse a little before four.

Once the boys were tucked into bed, Daphne took Louisa straight to the rape crisis center at Lenox Hill Hospital. Luckily, there had been no penetration, and since Louisa was eighteen, it was not mandatory to call the police. Bruised and frightened though she was, Louisa was able to talk to the counselor.

Holding tightly to Daphne's hand, she told the counselor that she was not quite asleep when Kenny launched his body on top of hers holding his hand over her mouth. In the struggle, a water pitcher overturned drenching them both, and Louisa had managed to hit him on the head with the telephone receiver before Daphne appeared.

Leaving Lenox Hill at six, Louisa told Daphne she did not want to go to the police station. Daphne supported her decision, as the NYPD never had a good reputation for kindness toward beautiful attempted rape victims. The questions seemed accusatory. Of course, penetration was another matter. Bundling Louisa up, Daphne put her arm around her, and they walked back to 70th Street in the half-light of early morning.

Louisa spent the next month at Daphne's mother's house, seeing a therapist three times a week. Daphne told her that she had to be strong and determined not to allow this experience to become part of her identity and assured Louisa she would be fine once she got back to London where no one had ever heard of Kenny Lang. Daphne had been right. Louisa was able to move on, but Daphne, irrationally, still blamed herself for what had happened that night.

Still unable to fall asleep, Daphne switched on her bedside lamp. It was only ten-thirty so she padded downstairs to the pantry, barefoot, to refill her wine glass. The bluish light from the refrigerator pooled around her in the dark kitchen. She stood still for a moment, enjoying the cool air on her bare skin, before reaching past the Welch's grape juice for the open bottle of Chardonnay. She filled the glass, but there was a little left, not enough to save. She slugged it back straight from the bottle. There was more than she reckoned and some dripped down her chin. Wiping it off with the back of her hand, she thought this would bring her to the sweet oblivion of sleep.

It didn't, though, and her problems cycled in her head. Kenny, Ella, lawyers, money, name change, broken window, work. Round and round it went. At midnight she went down again, opened another bottle and refilled her glass.

Chapter 3

By mid-October no traces of Gloria were left in Manhattan, and the city blazed in the glory of autumn. The air was cool and crisp, promising excitement, as Daphne made her way through Central Park toward her office. Her mind, flitting through subjects, ultimately landed on her job. She liked being in the jewelry design business, which thanks to Richard Blake, she'd fallen into a year ago, just a couple of months after her mother died.

Richard took Daphne to the Gemological Institute of America and enrolled her in a three-week course. He told her she needed to get out of the house and start bringing herself back to life for the boys' sake. Something clicked, and soon Daphne was working for Richard in Rockefeller Center and throwing herself into jewelry design. She clearly had a talent for this and, against all odds, was beginning to have some success, selling to Saks and Neiman's as well as fine jewelry stores in all parts of the country.

Daphne blew into her office in high spirits and saw the pink message slip on her desk. "Call your Uncle Ludlow in Thomasville", it said. He had been in Georgia for the past three days visiting his friends the Hamilton's and meeting with Ella Smyth and her lawyer.

She punched in the numbers written on the slip. "Hamilton Residence, good morning."

"May I speak to Mr. Fowler, please?" A few moments later, she heard the smoky voice rumbling at the other end of the phone. "Uncle Ludlow! I thought you'd have left by now. Is everything all right?"

"Everything's fine. It's just that Ella didn't want to see what I had to show her. She knew the truth. She just hoped we didn't and was very disappointed that I had proof that she is not your father's daughter."

Daphne sighed, leaned back in her chair and closed her eyes.

"Listen, Daphne. This young woman is well taken care of thanks to your father's generosity to her mother, and she's no blood relative of yours."

"I know, but still."

"'But still', nothing. Her mother was your father's mistress. They had a son together who died at birth and then her mother went on to another man. That other man is Ella's father. End of story."

"That's it?"

"As far as the law is concerned, it is. I showed Ella the letter her mother signed concerning paternity at the time of her birth. Your father was paying the rent, but he and Ella's mother had not seen each other in over a year. There is no way your father is her father. Your father gave Mrs. Smyth a generous amount of money at the time the boy who would have been your half-brother died, and that was the end of it. They never saw each other again, but the lease on the house your father was renting for her had two more years to go. He was paying the rent. That's all. When Ella was born I was worried that something like this could happen, so I had Mrs. Smyth sign a statement of paternity, absolving your father."

"It just seems so awful. When did her mother die?"

"A couple of years ago. You've got to realize this woman could have done a lot worse than meet your father. Thanks to him she could buy the house he'd been leasing for her or move anywhere in the world she wanted. He made her financially independent. That she stayed in Thomasville and had another child out of wedlock was not his call. I'm not saying it was the right thing to have the affair to begin with while he was married to your mother, but for Mrs. Smyth the advantages were huge. Don't forget that. He didn't seduce an innocent woman. She knew all along that he was a married man who had no intention of getting divorced, and she was happy with the arrangement they had between them. I happen to know that for a fact."

"I just never knew this side of him."

"There're a lot of men who're not perfect, Daphne."

"But this seems so sordid. Did my mother know about the whole thing?"

"I don't know the answer to that."

"But you could make an educated guess, right?" Daphne felt certain Ludlow knew more.

"I don't like to make suppositions. Darling Daphne, I'm sorry this is troubling you. But I've met with this young woman and, believe me, she is not the sentimental sort. She was looking for easy money. That's all."

"Does she need it?"

"She comes across as a surly, demanding girl and not overly successful. Her mother sent her to college, but she dropped out. Anyway, she owns the house her mother bought. Other than that, I don't know. It's none of my business. I just wanted to come to Thomasville personally to make sure that everything is completely clear. And it is. I met with Ella and her lawyer, and there is no question in their minds. It's over, Daphne."

"Uncle Ludlow, thank you so much for doing this. I was just hoping I had a nice half-sister in Thomasville."

"Well, you don't, Daphne. Please forget about this. I'm staying here in Georgia for lunch with my friends the Hamilton's and will take an early afternoon flight back. I'd love to have dinner with you tonight, if you're free. I'm going to stay in town."

"I'd love that. Just tell me where and when."

"How about the Knick at eight?"

"I'll be there."

Around four that afternoon, just before the boys came back from school, an efficient sounding woman called Daphne saying Mr. Case of the Wilson School was on the line for her. 'Which one is Mr. Case?' she wondered while waiting for him to come on the line. She recognized his voice as someone she had met on family night, but was not sure what his title was exactly. Someone important, though.

Carefully hanging up the phone after the conversation, Daphne put her elbows on her desk and held her head with her palms pressing into her temples. Trying to make sense of what she had just heard, she reviewed the call in her mind. Joe, the only one in kindergarten unable to read and Henry, using 'unacceptable language'. Maybe they are in the wrong kind of school was her first thought. Joe, not even six - give him a break, and Henry doesn't swear. At least not that she'd ever heard. What was this man talking about?

Daphne had never worried about her children's progress at school. In fact, she had never really had any reason to worry about the boys. Everyone had told her how well Henry and Joe seemed to have gotten through the divorce. They had seemed satisfied with the vague answers she and Marie had given them, and they were flexible. Look at how they took the name change in stride, she thought, gritting her teeth thinking of how much she'd had to pay Kenny for it. But why should something be wrong now? Hadn't she just talked to the school psychologist a month ago about the name change? He hadn't mentioned any problems. Possibly, this was all just a misunderstanding.

After dinner with Ludlow that evening, Daphne kissed the sleeping boys and poured herself a judicious amount of white wine in her favorite French wine glass. 'Piscine' they call this size glass in the Paris cafes, 'swimming pool'. Just as she was coming through the door of her bedroom, the phone rang. It was Maggie.

"Hey, what's doing in New York?" Not waiting for a reply, she started right in.

"It's been a day from hell here. I'll spare you the details, but let me guarantee you Chicago earns its title "the windy city". I'm having some people from the bank over on Saturday for brunch and have been making lots of Bloody Mary's. Damn, I'm good at this."

"It's only Thursday. And it sounds like you've been sampling."

"Since five."

"It's not good to drink alone, Maggie."

"Aren't you drinking alone right now, Daphne?"

"No. I'm having a glass of wine with you before I go to bed." Daphne could hear Maggie inhaling and imagined the stream of smoke rising like incense to the ceiling.

"Vodka wipes the smudges off my day, and it doesn't give a damn if I'm alone or not."

"I know what you mean. Since you moved, I don't drink unless I go out or if I'm on the phone with you. I miss it."

"Well, you don't get to miss it very often since we talk almost every night." Maggie was slurring her words slightly.

"It's only just a small glass of white wine," answered Daphne looking at the oversized 'piscine' in her hand.

"Oh, well, you're the expert on wine. Me, I go for the vodka. How the heck are you, anyway?"

"I've had a day from hell, too. The situation in Thomasville with this Ella woman still seems murky to me. Ludlow says it is crystal clear to him, but I don't know. And to top it off, I had a call from the head of lower school at Wilson saying things aren't going well for the boys. I haven't said anything to anyone about this yet. I guess I should go see the school psychologist again."

"Oh, Daphne. I'm so sorry about the boys, but you don't need to keep running to a psychologist. They'll be fine. They're stars. But what do you mean by the situation is murky in Thomasville?

Daphne went over what had happened and ended by saying, "I have to admit, I was hoping to discover a wonderful half-sister."

"Well, you've got a wonderful half-brother in Johnny."

"I do, but you know I'm much closer to Louisa. Johnny and Amelia are more my mother's vintage."

"Too bad for that Ella girl she called Johnny instead of you. How'd she get his number, anyway?"

"From the obit years ago. It said Johnny lives in London, and he's listed in the phone book."

"And what did the school say about the boys?"

"Let's not talk about it. I'm looking at the calendar right now, and my birthday is on a Wednesday."

"What?"

"Remember, you're going to try to come to New York for my birthday."

"Oh, yeah. I'm going to do that. Count me in."

"Call me tomorrow." Daphne hung up, took a Valium and was soon asleep.

The next morning, Daphne called and found that the school psychologist was on medical leave and not expected back in his office until the first week in November. Feeling like she had won a well-deserved reprieve, she called Mr. Case with a light heart.

"Mr. Case, unfortunately, the therapist is away for a couple of weeks so I cannot do anything about yesterday's conversation until he returns."

"Mrs. Hone, I appreciate that you have taken this seriously, but I don't think you need the therapist. You need to spend some time reading with Joe and possibly get a tutor. And as for Henry, you just have to sit him down and explain that certain words are inappropriate."

"I've never heard him say anything inappropriate, myself, so it'll be hard for me to reprimand him."

"Henry is a very smart boy. He'll understand. And Joe will catch up easily. I didn't mean to alarm you yesterday. I just don't want things to deteriorate. I'm confident you can handle this."

"Thank you, Mr. Case." Damn, she thought.

"Anything going on in the last year which might be affecting the boys?"

"The divorce was final a year ago, as you know, and we are just legalizing the name change from Lang to Hone. Neither Henry nor Joe seemed to care about that at all. I did talk to the psychologist about how to handle it before I mentioned it to them, but as it turned out, they didn't even bat an eye."

"Do they still see their father every weekend?"

"Only if he shows up before eleven on Saturdays. Sometimes this is too difficult for him. He manages an art gallery in Soho that's open on the weekend."

"I see. There's nothing consistent, then?"

"I can't do anything about the law, Mr. Case. My ex-husband has the legal right to see the boys every Saturday and certain holidays. In the beginning I never knew if he would arrive at eight a.m. or five p.m., and Henry and Joe were waiting around all day. So, now, he forfeits his right to see them if he doesn't pick them up by eleven."

"Not knowing must be hard for them."

"They're flexible, like most kids, and I always have something planned if their father doesn't show."

"Well, good luck, Mrs. Hone. Let us know if there is anything we can do to help."

"Everything is fine, really. But thank you for your concern." Daphne made a face at the phone and hung up.

The next Monday night, after reading with Joe, Daphne came into their bathroom as the boys were brushing their teeth, each standing on a little stool. There were two pottery mugs on the shelf. Joe reached over for a mug to rinse his mouth. "Hey, that's my mug, you ugly fucker," Henry said in an ordinary tone of voice.

"Henry!" Daphne was surprised but could hardly keep a straight face.

"What, Mom?"

"Don't ever use words like that!"

"What words?"

"Uncle Richard will talk to you. He'll tell you."

"Whatever."

"Henry, that's rude, saying 'whatever' like that."

"Okay, Mom. Sorry. But Dad talks like that."

"You're not Dad."

Daphne went to the sink and put an arm around each of them and hugged them tightly. "You guys are the best, and I'm sorry if I sounded angry. I just want you to beware that words are important. They can mean things you don't expect them to mean. You're hearing new words everyday, and I want you to use them correctly. Swear words have no place in this house or at school." Daphne kissed the top of each head.

Half an hour later and Daphne was laughingly recounting the scene in the bathroom to Maggie. She could hear Maggie's ice tinkling cheerfully in the glass. Daphne looked at her own drink. Silent, but deadly, she thought.

"I dread having to talk to Kenny about this."

"Being a single mother isn't easy, Daphne. Come to think of it, I don't like being single myself. But now, get a load of this." Maggie's voice was shrill.

"What?"

"I got a DUI last night. *Un*believable. I had almost nothing to drink. I'm sure the test is rigged."

"What happened?"

"I rented a car after work yesterday since I had bank business in Lake Forest early this morning. I stopped off at Cricket's on my way home last night to have a few drinks with friends from the bank, and as I was parking, *right* outside my building, not one but *two* cop cars flashed their red lights. And poor me, all alone in the car. What could I do but take their stupid test?"

"What's the test?"

"Oh, I had to walk and turn and that was fine. Then I had to stand on one leg. Well, in three-inch spikes, no one could do that. So I failed. Then I had to touch my forefinger to my nose. But I was flustered because I'd stumbled on the one-legged test so I failed that as well. Bastards. That's when they had me breathe into that hand-held thing."

"Then what happened?"

"They *arrested* me, took me down to the station, booked me and found out by super-computer methods known only to the police that I got a speeding ticket in Connecticut this past May, which I didn't pay. Somehow the paper work got lost between here and there. They took my license, and now I have to go to court next month."

"Oh, my God, Maggie."

"That's not all. I had to get a car with a driver to take me to my meeting in Lake Forest. Can you imagine? How embarrassing is that?"

"What'd you say about showing up in a chauffeur driven car?"

"I said, 'I'm a New Yorker and don't drive.' And that would've been okay except some smart-ass remembered my parents live in Connecticut."

"And?"

"Oh, I managed to laugh it off, but then at the end of the day, when I had to get the rented car back, the agent wanted to see my license to *return* the car – have you ever heard of anything so idiotic? And he was curious that I had only driven it for six miles."

"What'd you say?"

"I had to lie and say my wallet was stolen, and my license was in it, and I didn't want to drive their precious car without a license. These crazy people out here are so anxious to be helpful, the agent actually wanted to report this to the police for me. Really! It was all I could do to get out of there with my sanity."

"This could only happen to you, Maggie." Daphne shook her head, smiling.

"But now, I'm embarrassed to ask the bank's lawyer to represent me. Will you ask your Uncle Ludlow to give me the name of someone out here?"

"Sure."

"The bank doesn't have to be privy to every little thing in my private life."

"Of course not. None of their business."

"You don't think this will get into the paper, do you?" Maggie's voice was weak.

"Certainly not in the financial section. So many worse things happen in Chicago."

"I could always say it was my birthday."

"Don't. Too easy to check. Say it was someone else's bachelorette party."

"I can't. I was with these people from the bank."

"Oh, Maggie, don't worry. Nothing will happen. I'll call you tomorrow with the name of someone reliable."

Next morning, it was Maggie again on the phone, "Daphne, get this. People in Chicago actually read the Police Blotter. Everyone knows, but no one seems to mind. It's too weird. In New York I would be called on the carpet for this, but here it's like I joined their club or something. Colleagues are patting me on the back, and even the big boss here, Mr. O'Reilly, just walked by my desk and said, 'Take it easy, Miller.' Can you beat that?"

"I'll get Uncle Ludlow's contact for you. I've got another call. Speak to you later." Daphne's thoughts were elsewhere. Although she was interested in everything in Maggie's life, today she couldn't concentrate. There was too much going on. One of the things she wanted to do was to organize her birthday.

Daphne called Herman Agar for two Orchestra seats, third row center, for 'The Iceman Cometh'. Telling her how difficult that would be, as he always did, he called back in fifteen minutes saying he had managed to get them, as he always did, at an eye-popping price, but, well, it was her thirty-second birthday.

Richard vaguely remembered her birthday was coming up and asked what she was planning. "Maggie's coming from Chicago for the night, and we're going to 'Iceman' and then to Trader Vic's."

"I can't believe they can sell tickets to that. Gloomy and awful."

"Are you kidding? It has fantastic reviews."

"Critics like to be depressed. You and Maggie go and have a good time, and I'll meet you at Trader Vic's when it's over."

"Good idea."

"And how about dinner tonight? I could come to your house for Marie's famous home cooking and some games with Henry and Joe."

"Fine. Come at six-thirty. Something happened at school, and I want to talk to you about it after dinner." Daphne was used to Richard's last minute plans and was always pleased when that meant his spending time with her and the boys. Though only eight years older than Daphne, Richard had been her mother's friend and had watched with Daphne as her life ebbed away. Their shared grief forged a strong bond between them. Richard was always there for her during the divorce, listening and advising. Many of his evenings were spent with Daphne and Ludlow during that traumatic time. He loved Henry and Joe and showed it by spending quality time with them.

Leaving work at four o'clock that day, Daphne stopped by the Emanuel Ungaro boutique on Madison Avenue to look for something fashionable to wear to the theatre on her birthday. She decided on a scarlet velvet suit with a straight skirt and powerful pleated shoulders. It had a shocking pink and purple satin shell to wear underneath. She loved it and already had just the right shoes in her closet.

Richard arrived as the pot roast was being served, a bottle of cold Champagne under one arm and a large box of Teuscher's chocolates under the other. At six-foot-two Richard paunch, which he complained about constantly, but did nothing to diminish. It looked like he might end up a perennial bachelor, though he had had several notorious entanglements with high-profile women. Daphne had read about his private life on Page Six of the New York Post, but he never mentioned what the whole world knew.

"What do your girlfriends think about you coming over here all the time?"

"What girlfriends? I don't have any girlfriends."

"You never tell me anything. I have to read about it on Page Six."

"I'm always surprised by what I read." Richard said wearily.

"Oh, Richard." Daphne knew he was a tomb of discretion. Though she wanted to know all about Richard's love life, she knew that door was closed to her. But she knew she could count on his loyalty and love for her and the boys. She knew this beyond a shadow of a doubt.

After dinner, Daphne said, "Let's skip dessert and take the chocolates into the library with the rest of the Champagne." She cocked her head and looked at the bottle. "Actually, there's almost none left, I'll crack a fresh one."

The boys were already playing their favorite math game with Richard in the library when Daphne came in with the Champagne. Richard gave out dollars for correct answers. Daphne didn't know what she thought about that, but the three of them were having a good time, and she didn't want to interrupt. Chugger, the boxer puppy, wanted to join in, but since his math skills were poor, Richard tucked the dollars in his collar so he could deliver them to the lucky winners. Jazz, the cat, looked on from the back of the sofa with feline disdain.

Too soon it was time for baths and bed, and Richard went up and read to the boys. Daphne stayed downstairs. Glazed with Champagne, she flipped thought art books looking for inspiration for her jewelry designs.

Richard returned and sat by her side. "Tell me what the teacher said."

"It's worse than that. It's the head of lower school, and he said Henry has been using the 'f' word, and Joe is not reading as well as the others in his class."

"Have they overheard you talking about this Ella Smyth woman?"

"I don't think so. Why?"

"Oh, you know, kids pick up on how you're feeling. I know that's been on your mind. Just wondering. They're such great kids. I'll talk to Henry about the 'f' word and help Joe with the reading."

"Thanks, Richard. What would I do without you?"

Richard stood up and shrugged on his trench coat. "Delicious dinner. Thanks. I'll come back tomorrow. Don't worry about the boys. Sleep tight."

After taking the wine cooler up to her room, Daphne kissed the sleeping boys and called Maggie.

"Did you get the name and number I left for you?"

"Yes. Sid Weiss. Thank your Uncle Ludlow for me. I guess I'd better check in with him tomorrow. What's going on in New York? Any news about Ella Smyth or from the school?"

"Nothing new. Richard came over for dinner, bringing chocolates and generally spoiling the boys. He said he'd talk to Henry. And help Joe. I'm so lucky to have a friend like that."

"Maybe he'd like to be more than a friend."

"Oh, *please.* I've known him way too long. And, believe me, he would never be interested in me. I'm not glamorous enough."

"Well, you are, and you just never know. And like I tell you every week, the boys need a good father. The one they have is unfit for the job. Richard would make a great father, you have to admit."

"God, Maggie you're such a romantic. I've got tickets for 'The Iceman Cometh' for us on my birthday. And that Romeo Richard will join us at Trader Vic's afterwards. Did you get your plane ticket?"

"So excited to see 'Iceman'. Everyone here is talking about it. And, yes, I have my ticket. I arrive at LaGuardia at four p.m. your time on Wednesday and leave on the seven a.m. flight on Thursday."

"I'm so glad you're coming. Lionel will pick you up at baggage claim. The boys will be sorry you're not staying longer." Maggie was their honorary aunt. They called her Magpie, and she loved them.

"Me, too. But tell them I'll be back at Thanksgiving."

Chapter 4

The morning of Daphne's birthday Marie helped Henry and Joe bring pancakes up to her room at seven and they all sang 'Happy Birthday'. Marie had to rush them off to school, but Daphne promised to pick them up and bring them home for ice cream and cake.

Once the boys had gone, Daphne stretched and snuggled into her bed. Louisa called from London to wish her happy birthday. And just as she was going out the door for work, Fred pulled up delivering a distinctive robin's egg blue Tiffany box for her from Ludlow. As she walked toward mid-town, she thought how lucky she was to have such loving family and friends. Daphne was happy, and she couldn't wait to see Maggie.

Unusually warm for early November, but cloudy, the day raced by, and Daphne had already blown out the candles on her cake and had opened her Tiffany box. She already had on the Elsa Peretti open heart necklace by the time Maggie arrived. Lionel took the suitcase upstairs. He would wait and take them to the theatre and then on to Trader Vic's in the basement of the Plaza Hotel before he went home that night.

Daphne and Maggie loved the play and left the theatre, cheeks streaked with mascara. Lionel was waving a flashlight so it was easy to spot Daphne's station wagon. It was a huge green thing with simulated wood panels, which stood out in the sea of black limos and yellow taxis.

When the two women arrived at Trader Vic's, Richard was sipping a scotch and looking over the menu. He glanced up and said, "You girls look beautiful. I certainly hope there's someone in here taking note of me with two such stunning women." Daphne looked at Maggie as if seeing her with new eyes. 'Yes,' she thought, 'Maggie *is* absolutely lovely. Four inches taller than I am, with that precisely cut black hair and peaches and cream skin. She does lope along in such a boyish way, though, boney shoulders rolling out in front. But one of the best things about Maggie is her total lack of self-awareness. And her kindness.' Daphne thought about all the years they'd known each other and how Maggie's kindness was one thing she could always count on.

Daphne snatched the menu from Richard and told the waiter to bring them a Pupu platter, a double order of Cheese Bings and one Scorpion for four with two gardenias and three straws.

"This woman knows how to take charge." Richard lit Maggie's cigarette. "So how's Chicago treating you, Maggie?"

"I'm not sure. The people are the nicest in the world, but I don't fit in." Maggie slouched on the banquette. "Did Daphne tell you I got a DUI?"

"No. But no New Yorker can tell if it's okay to drive or not. We just don't have the instinct for it like others do."

"Thanks, Richard, I'll remember that and not drive. Not that there's any chance of that. They relieved me of my license, which is a real pain. It's my I.D."

"That's about all I use mine for, except in the summer. It seems I only drive in the summer. Only when I'm going out of town."

By the time Trader Vic's thinned out, around midnight, Daphne and Maggie each had two gardenias. Richard invited them to Double's, the private nightclub, for Champagne. They left the Plaza by the side door and walked past several Hansom cabs on the way to the Sherry Netherland Hotel. Once they got down the red staircase, Richard had a word with François and ordered a birthday cake for Daphne.

They walked to the back of the nightclub, waving to acquaint-ances, and sat by the dance floor. "I don't think I should have any Champagne," Maggie said. "I have an early flight in the morning. And I can tell, if there were a car here, I shouldn't be the one driving it."

Richard said, "You can have Mimosas. The orange juice cancels out the alcohol." God knows where he got that misinformation - maybe he just made it up. He ordered two Mimosas and a Calvados and put his arm around Maggie. "Now, don't you worry about driving tonight, Maggie. If there's anything I hate, it's to see a beautiful woman worried about having to drive around New York City at night."

The cake came and went, and it was two o'clock when the three of them finally climbed the stairs from Doubles. "Look. There's a perfect half-moon. I'll walk you girls home." They laughed as they stumbled back to Daphne's and went in for a nightcap. Richard left when the first streaks of gold were lighting the sky. "It's after five. Can you believe it?" wailed Maggie.

"Don't worry. I'll make coffee and bacon and eggs. Lionel will be here soon to pick you up. Go pack your things, and I'll cook." Daphne felt woozy.

"You're so lucky to work for Richard, Daphne. I don't know how I'll get through the day." Maggie walked gingerly up the stairs, hanging on to the brass rail. She looked at herself in the bathroom mirror and shivered.

Fifteen minutes later Henry came into the kitchen, lured by the smell of bacon. Daphne tried to give him a hug, but he pushed her away.

"Your breath smells yucky, Mom. It's that gross wine. I hate it."

"It's not the wine. Maggie smokes non-stop. You're just not used to the smell." Daphne stirred the eggs with a fork. "Want some scrambled eggs, Honey?" Her tongue felt too big for her mouth.

"No, that's okay." He reached for a crisp strip of bacon and left the kitchen.

After Maggie left for the airport and the boys went to school, Daphne went to bed and felt pretty good, considering. When she came-to around four that afternoon, she realized she'd taken a couple of Valiums before going to sleep. She knew this was dangerous, but it seemed like the prudent thing to do at the time. As it turned out, she had slept through her two p.m. meeting with Mr. Case. Quickly she flipped though her address book and found the number for the Wilson School.

"Mr. Case, this is Daphne Hone, and I'm so sorry to have missed our appointment. I had an emergency at work. I'm only now able to get to a phone. Please accept my sincerest apology."

"This is unfortunate, Mrs. Hone. I'm anxious to see you so please re-schedule at your earliest convenience. I look forward to seeing you." The connection was cut, but Daphne continued to hold the receiver to her ear until the dial tone jolted her out of her daze. People's lives don't revolve around the school, she thought, consoling herself. She would call and reschedule tomorrow, but really, the rudeness of this man hanging up on her like that. They take themselves so seriously, these school people. Daphne sulked.

That night Maggie called at eight to say she'd arrived safely. "I'm already in bed nursing my hangover. Every *single* strand of hair on my head hurts, and I can't even remember what happened after we got back to your house."

"Nothing happened. We just drank a little too much."

"Never again for me. Tomorrow I'm turning over a new leaf. I may even give up smoking."

"Stranger things have happened, Maggie, but not many."

That was the last Daphne ever heard about Maggie's quitting smoking, and the day after Thanksgiving they met in the Palm Court at the Plaza Hotel for tea. The boys came along for cocoa and a close-up look at Eloise's portrait. There were several violists playing, and potted palms screened off the rest of the world. The opulent old-world setting was a favorite refuge for New Yorkers who were exhausted from shopping at Bergdorf's, and every gilded chair was taken.

"Who is that elegant older woman smoking with the cigarette holder? Do you know?" Maggie inhaled deeply as the waiter lit her cigarette.

Daphne turned and looked over her shoulder. "Oh, my God, it's Arabella Yamada. She came to see my mother practically every day that last year. I'm going to say hello. Be right back. She has the *most* romantic story."

Daphne approached the table, noticing the perfect posture and serene grace of the older woman. "Madame Yamada, I'm Daphne Hone."

"Of course. How lovely to see you, Daphne. I think of you and your boys often, and your mother, your dear mother, how I miss her."

"I wish you would come and see us. The boys and I would love that. Last year, I called the Asia Society for your number, but no one wanted to give it to me."

"I live at the Sherry Netherland Hotel now, but you can find me here almost every day at tea time. Are you still living in your mother's enchanting house?" Arabella kept her silver hair short and close to her head.

"Yes, we are still on 70th Street. I'm so happy to see you, and please expect a call from me soon. The boys are here and my school friend Maggie Miller. Won't you join us?"

"Normally, I would love to, but today I have a guest, but please call me, I would love see you again, dear. I do have a private telephone, but you can just call the hotel number anytime, and they will put you through to me."

Having spent Thanksgiving Day with her parents in Greenwich, Maggie was looking forward to spending that Friday night at Daphne's. Both women thought of the last evening they spent together and neither wanted a repeat. Just a night home with the boys was what they both wanted.

After Henry and Joe had gone to sleep, Daphne and Maggie went to the library to sit by the fire and chat. "Fix yourself a drink." Daphne filled the ice bucket. "I forgot to ask you, what's happening with your court date?"

"It's next week. My mother handed me a pile of mail, which was mostly reminders of my speeding ticket. Anyway, all that's taken care of now, and Sid Weiss is great, by the way. He doesn't think there'll be any problem getting my license back now that the speeding ticket's paid. I'm a cooperative first offender, after all. There might be a small fine, but that's it."

"Thank goodness for that."

"Now, tell me about Arabella Yamada. You said there's a fascinating story."

Daphne took a deep breath. "Sometime in the mid 1960s, my mother met her at an Asia Society board meeting. Even though Mom was much younger, they slowly became friends, and at the end, Madame Yamada was her closest and most loyal companion. She's a wonderful woman, and I'm intrigued by her so I found out as much as I could."

"Give me the Cliff Notes."

"This is what I've pieced together from what Mom told me and what Arabella said about herself. First of all, she's a lot older than she looks. I think she was born around 1900 in San Francisco. I know looking at her, it's hard to believe she's eighty-five, but I'm pretty sure I'm right on that."

"She's lovely. I would never have guessed more than late-sixties." Maggie slipped her shoes off and tucked her feet under her burying them in the soft down of the chintz-covered armchair.

"When she was eighteen, she fell in love with a Japanese boy named Yoshinori Ando just at the end of the First World War. It was love at first sight, literally, and they saw each other secretly for six months before her father found out. Then there was a big scene, and her father somehow must have used his power to have Yoshi arrested on a trumped-up robbery charge, and he ended up being deported. Tough, I know, but those kinds of things happened in those days."

"Terrible."

"Yes. But Arabella didn't know this. She thought Yoshi had ditched her."

"She obviously has a Japanese last name and not his. What happened?"

"Well, she never married and after her father died, she went off to Japan, just as a tourist, but thinking she might find Yoshi. His family was easy enough to track down as the Ando clan is ancient and well known, but she always ran into a brick wall. No one could remember a Yoshinori Ando who went to Stanford. She went to Japan year after year and eventually gave up asking about him. Then, in 1965, she went on an Asia Society trip and was staying in Hakone at a hotel and saw him. She saw him right there in the hotel lobby. They looked at each other, and it was love at first sight all over again. He had never married but had never dared come back for her. He thought she believed he was a thief, just as his own father had."

"What do you mean?"

"When he was deported from the U. S. on that robbery charge, his father disowned him, and Yoshi took on the name of Yamada, which is like Smith or Jones. He did well in business, though, and became a wealthy man in his own right. But a man without a clan in Japan is very difficult. Anyway, he had never looked at another woman and just threw himself into his work. Then he retired and took a trip to the spa at Hakone. And there she was right in front of him."

"This story is giving me goose bumps. Do you think we'll ever have such a romance?"

"I don't know, but guess what. They got married right away and moved to New York. They had ten years of blissful happiness, and then he dropped dead one afternoon after walking the dogs in the park."

"Strange story. But how wonderful they found each other and at least had those ten years together."

"My mother said they were like young lovers, always holding hands, leaving parties early, et cetera. He was handsome, too."

"Did you ever meet him?"

"No, but I saw photographs of them. I only got to know her after I moved back home two years ago. I think she's a mystery to most people. My mother was one of her few friends."

"Why do you call her Madame Yamada?"

"I have no idea. I guess I was introduced to her that way. I'm sure she wouldn't mind if you called her Mrs. Yamada."

"Oh, I don't care. Just wondering. Do you think I'll get the chance to meet her?"

"I hope to see a lot of her. I thought I'd lost her. Wouldn't it be nice for the boys to have a granny-type figure in their lives? With their Lang grandparents moving to Tucson they won't be seeing much of them. Of course, they have Uncle Ludlow, but no older woman, and she has no family of her own. She might like to spend some time with us."

Maggie sighed and stretched. "I'd love to meet her. I'd love to hear more of her story. In fact, I would like to have a story of my own. Oh, Daphne, look at us, two attractive women in our early thirties. Where are the men?"

"I know what you mean. Actually, I'd have been better off with an arranged marriage."

"You can say that again."

"And Mom never found anyone after Dad died. Richard was her escort to a lot of things."

"Sad your Dad died so young. We had so much fun with him. Will you ever forget that trip to Yellowstone? With the bear suit? He was the best."

"That he was. I still miss him." Daphne yawned. "I'll make sure you meet Madame Yamada. It's been great being with you tonight, Magpie. Henry and Joe have missed you. And me, too."

Chapter 5

Back in Chicago, Maggie met with Sid Weiss on the day before her court appearance. Ludlow was right about his style of dressing. The white shoes and striped jacket were surprising. "Look, Maggie, we've got bad luck with the judge. You may not get your license back after all. We've got Marsha Allen, and she can't stand drunk drivers. Tell you what I want you to do. Dress neat and tidy, and walk in there with your head down. Let me handle the rest."

"Okay. Where will I meet you?"

"Come here at eight thirty; we'll walk over there together. No big deal. You're a first offender, and you don't look like a troublemaker. Just leave all the talking to me."

"What do you think will happen with this judge?"

"She's not going to throw the book at you or anything, but I doubt you'll get your license back right away. She's not happy to have drunks driving around on the streets of Chicago."

"But I was just parking the car."

"Yeah, I know. We'll mention that." Sid crumpled up a paper on his desk, leaned back in his swivel chair and tossed it nonchalantly into the wastebasket, signaling to Maggie that her time was up for today.

Judge Marsha Allen was a good looking, petite brunette, but once she was robed and sitting on the bench her mouth formed a thin down-turned line. She looked at Maggie over her half-moon glasses and sized her up. After hearing all the particulars of the case. She said, "Suspension of license, three months. Probation, one year.

$500 fine." She slammed her gavel so hard Maggie felt like it slapped her in the face, burning her cheeks with rage.

Sid touched Maggie's shoulder. "Walk me back to my office. You look like you could use some fresh air."

Maggie pressed her lips together. Outrage was leaking out of the sides of her mouth.

Sensing her mood, Sid said, "Look, Maggie. You don't have to be mad at the judge. She's just doing her job. You were the one operating a vehicle under the influence."

Maggie did not reply. She walked by Sid's side all the way out of the courthouse. On the street, she turned to Sid, "What a weird town you live in. Police arresting people for parking cars. Judges who hate hard-working citizens. "

Sid looked tired. "This is just how it works, Maggie. If the police happen to see a car being parked in an unusual manner, they investigate. If the driver is intoxicated, this is the consequence. Nothing personal. Just what happens. Drawing Judge Allen was a bit of hard luck, but other than that, this is routine."

"For your information, I had less to drink than anyone else at Cricket's that night. Why would *I* be the one to get caught, and why did I get *that* judge."

"It's okay, Maggie. Go home or go to work and call me tomorrow. I'll take care of the details."

"I'm just so angry."

"I can tell."

Sid hailed a cab for Maggie and gave the driver her home address. Maggie sat in silence for the fifteen-minute drive. She barely acknowledged the doorman, unlocked her door and headed straight for the phone. "Oh, my God, Daphne, I almost lost control at the sentencing."

"What happened, Maggie? You sound like you're calling from underwater."

Maggie cleared her throat. "I could've started screaming. I could've torn into that judge. I mean, I really could've bitten her or something."

"What are you talking about?"

"When she banged her gavel, something snapped in me. I was on the verge of madness, like dizzy with rage. All I can say is I'm really glad I have such strong self-control. I needed every bit not to lash out and end up with an assault conviction. I never would have dreamed I could feel like that. It was scary."

"Did you tell Sid Weiss?"

"Of course not."

"I'm only asking because maybe it's normal to feel like that. What's the sentence?"

"Probation for a year. Imagine, I'll have a probation officer! I can't believe that and the way she looked at me with complete disgust when she slammed her gavel down. I really need a drink. I'll fix one and call you back in a few minutes."

"Look, Maggie, you need a friend, not a drink. I'm going to book a flight to Chicago right now. Go to work. I'll be there in time for dinner. I'll sleep on your sofa for a few nights."

Relief flooded Maggie's mind and body. "Oh, Daphne. Thank you so much. I do need you to be here, but what about the boys?"

"Marie can handle everything better than anyone, including me. She's the best. I'm so lucky and so are the boys. See you this evening."

"I'll leave my key with the doorman just in case you get here before I'm back from the bank. You're an angel to come, Daphne. Please hurry. I feel raw. This has really gotten to me."

The last rays of the autumn sun glazed the city skyline in shades of violet and gold as Daphne's taxi headed toward Lake Shore Drive. She had never been to Chicago and though she had seen pictures of its architectural marvels, the reality dazzled her. Tomorrow, she thought, I'll walk the famous Miracle Mile and see what that's all about.

Maggie's doorman greeted Daphne by name and said Maggie was in and expecting her.

Maggie was standing at the elevator. "Daphne, I'm so relieved to see you."

"And I'm glad to see you're still in one piece. What a time you've had!" The two women hugged each other and walked across the hall to Maggie's apartment.

"I took the afternoon off." Maggie dumped Daphne's bag on the sofa. "And I've made creamed chicken, rice and peas for supper. Remember? It was always birthday party dinner when we were little. I wish I could've found those squares of Neapolitan ice cream we used to have. No luck on that front, but I've got a quart of Häagen-Dazs chocolate."

"Sounds just right."

"This apartment came with twin beds. So you won't have to sleep on the sofa, and I made a couple of inches for you in my closet."

"So glad we're staying in tonight, and having my favorite comfort food. Let me have a shower and put on my pj's."

"What a good idea. Dinner will be ready when you get out of the shower and after dinner we can get into our beds and talk 'til we go to sleep, like when we were kids."

Maggie hummed to herself as she finished cooking the meal. This creamed chicken, this old friend were exactly what the doctor ordered.

Daphne came into the kitchen, "I didn't have a chance to tell you about the meeting at the school."

"What happened?"

"When I rescheduled with Mr. Case, he said he would like both parents at the meeting. So I told Kenny, and as I was waiting just outside Mr. Case's office, one of the teachers came in and said Mr. Lang was outside and wanted to see me. I looked out the window and could see Kenny standing beside a taxi and knew he was expecting me to pay the fare."

"Typical. You must've been furious."

"Not furious exactly. More distressed. What kind of model is he for Henry and Joe?"

"I know how hard this is on you, but you'll marry a nice man. You'll see."

"I love Henry and Joe with all my heart, and sometimes I feel so inadequate, like I can't be what I should be. Like an imposter."

"Oh, Daphne, stop. You are a wonderful mother. Love is what it's all about and you've got plenty of that."

The next morning the two women planned to meet at the restaurant in the old Marshall Field store in the Loop, near Maggie's bank.

Maggie was already seated when Daphne arrived with two shopping bags from Ultimo. "Here, Mag. This bag is for you."

"Oh, my God. You're kidding."

"No. Open it."

Maggie pulled out a very small and glittery black dress. "Oh, my God, Daphne, you shouldn't have! Totally fabulous, though. I love it!"

"So try it out tonight. I made a reservation for us at Le Ciel Bleu tonight. I hear it has the best view in town."

"It should have, and I've never been. What a treat!

That night, going up in the elevator to the eighteenth floor, Daphne turned to Maggie and laughed as she looked at their reflection in the elevator mirror.

"Look at us! We look like such New Yorkers in our black dresses. Do you think they will seat us in the tourist section?"

"No way. We look great." Maggie turned and looked over her shoulder to check out the back of her new dress.

The first thing Daphne did when they got to the table was order a bottle of Cristal Champagne. The girls looked around the elegant restaurant and admired the view which was much more intimate than views from taller buildings. The glamorous 1920s architecture set the ambiance and every detail was clean and crisp from the white tablecloths to the sparkling wine glasses and tail-coated waiters.

While waiting for the Champagne to arrive, Maggie turned to Daphne, "I don't know if we are being stared at because we're two women alone or because we're wearing such fashionable dresses or what. But this is making me uncomfortable." Maggie looked around the room defiantly.

"Don't go and get paranoid on me now, Maggie. Nobody's looking at us."

"Can't you feel their eyes on us?"

"You're just still overwrought from being at court yesterday. It's okay. No one is staring at us. I promise. Let's talk about the holidays. Are your parents still planning to come here?"

"Yes. And since I don't have a car, I don't think they'll ever have to know I don't have a license. Right?"

"Where are they going to stay?"

"At the Drake. Just around the corner from me. We passed it walking over here."

The waiter poured the Champagne and taking a sip, Daphne said, "Why don't you come to New York for a few days and stay with me after they leave?"

"Okay. I'd like that. I'll come for a few days right after New Year's." Maggie seemed calmer. "I'd love you to meet Sid Weiss before you leave. He's a real character. I can't tell you how grateful I am to Ludlow for giving me his name."

"I was hoping we could go to the Art Institute tomorrow. Can we meet him for lunch somewhere near there?"

"I doubt that would be convenient for him, but I'll call. He's a no-nonsense kind of guy, and I bet he'll be at his office tomorrow. We could stop by in the morning with some coffee. I think he'd like that."

"Good. We'll do it. So, Maggie, are we going to order a bottle of wine with dinner or should we be good?"

"Why don't we have wine with dinner? And I'll make green tea for us when we get back to my place."

Once back at the apartment, Maggie hopped up on the kitchen counter to reach the teapot in the cabinet above the refrigerator. The pot was camel-shaped with a wicker handle.

"That teapot's a riot. Where did you get it?" Daphne helped Maggie down.

"Oh, you know, it was one of those things I just *had* to have. It started life in this apartment as a vase, but since I have so few flowers, it migrated to the top shelf. This is the first time I've used it for actual tea." She rinsed the camel in the sink.

Maggie fussed around and found a tray, two cups with matching saucers, but couldn't seem to put her hand on the tea. Eventually the tea was found in a squashed, but unopened, box. Daphne put the kettle on.

Maggie opened the rectangular box of green tea bags. She sniffed them suspiciously and held it up for Daphne to smell. "Smells like hay," Maggie said.

"It always smells like that, Maggie. I don't think unopened tea gets stale."

Maggie got out three tea bags, draped them in the pot and looked over at the kettle.

Daphne caught the wary look. "It's much easier to drink wine than tea."

"But we had the wine. Now it's time to stand around and wait for the water to boil."

Finally, the two women were seated on the living room sofa sipping weak green tea.

"Tell me more about Sid Weiss. Uncle Ludlow has a lot of respect for him." Daphne sipped her tea.

"Have they actually met?"

"I think so, and they've done quite a bit of business together over the past few years, he told me."

"Well, Sid's great. I like him a lot. He's got a heart of gold and an unusual wardrobe and seems to be very well-known in Chicago."

"How was he in court?"

"You know, he warned me about the judge. How harsh she is. He clearly has her number, and he was totally great in court. Very professional, except, maybe the clothes. But his clothes suit his personality so well that after the first time you see him, they don't seem surprising. It would be weird to see him in a gray suit."

"I can't wait to meet him." Daphne put her cup and saucer on the table.

"Well, you will tomorrow. This tea tastes gross. How can people drink this stuff?" Maggie made a face.

"We really shouldn't be sitting here drinking tea and talking about Sid Weiss when we could be drinking wine and talking about more interesting things."

"I don't have any wine or Champagne or beer, but I bet I have the ingredients for a Grasshopper."

"What's that?"

"It's a New Orleans specialty involving green Crème de Menthe, Crème de Cacao and cream. I may not have any cream left, but we can improvise."

Maggie rummaged around in her kitchen, found the Crème de Menthe, but not the other two ingredients.

"I'll create a new drink. The Green Maggie. 'Pour half of a cup of Crème de Menthe and half of a cup of Vodka into the blender. Add eleven ice cubes and blend until slushy.' How does that sound?"

"Delicious. This could be a new career for you, Magpie." Daphne realized too late she should not be encouraging Maggie. Oh, well, one or two Green Maggie's won't throw the earth off its axis.

Chapter 6

Maggie arrived in New York with her suitcases as planned on January 2nd. The taxi pulled up in front of Daphne's house where she and the boys were waiting and rushed out to help Maggie with her things.

"I was so lucky to get out of Chicago before the storm. They were already canceling flights. So good to see you guys. So good to be in New York." Maggie hugged them all, went upstairs to the guest room and settled in.

"So is there anything special you want to do while you're in New York?" Daphne asked when she brought in a cup of tea.

"Just spend time with you and the boys. The only other thing I have planned is dinner tomorrow night with Richard."

"Richard? My Richard?"

"Oh, I never told you? We've talked a few times on the phone. And when he found out I was coming to New York, he said we should get together.

"Why haven't you told me about this?"

"There's not much to tell. He's a nice guy, isn't he? But tonight I want to invite you and the boys to Serendipity for foot-long hot dogs and frozen hot chocolate. It's really my favorite hot spot. Nothing like it in Chicago."

The next night, Daphne had no plans for herself so after reading to the boys and getting them tucked in, she stuck a bottle of white wine into a cooler and headed for her bedroom. The thought of her friends out without her! Was she interested in Richard for herself? No.

Definitely not. So why was she so upset by this? *I'm just a selfish bitch*, she thought as she switched on the classic movie channel, and by the time she heard Richard and Maggie come in, she noticed a second bottle of wine was standing nearly empty on her bedside table. She carefully lowered the empty one into the Lucite wastebasket in her bathroom, then slipped on a black velour tracksuit, sprayed Diorissimo perfume all around herself, fluffed up her hair, and went downstairs.

Daphne found them in the library. "Did you guys have any fun tonight?" She thought she might have caught them about to kiss. "Let's have a drink in the living room and listen to the juke box."

"Daphne, have you been crying?" Maggie asked.

"Just watching old movies. They always make me cry."

"What would you girls like? I'll tend the bar." Richard glanced at Maggie over Daphne's head.

"Bellini's," Daphne answered with enthusiasm.

In the living room, behind the Chinese screen, Daphne punched in a dozen of her favorite songs on the jukebox. Soon she and Maggie were singing along with Aretha Franklin when Richard returned and put the tray of Bellini's down. Daphne could feel Richard watching them and as the evening wore on, she sensed he was willing her to go to bed, but she was having too good a time. Maggie was her friend, not Richard's. After all, those two had been out together all night, and she had been home alone. Time for her to join the fun.

The next morning Maggie awoke to the boys peering at her. She was snug in the guest room, alone in a twin bed wearing her plaid flannel nightshirt. "Good morning, Magpie," they chimed. "Uncle Richard is downstairs looking for you. He said you promised to make pancakes."

"Tell him I'll be down in a minute. You guys get started cracking the eggs." Henry took Joe by the hand and left the room.

Maggie pulled herself together in less than five minutes. Minty-mouthed and cheery, she knocked on Daphne's door. "Up. Up, Daphne. Richard's already back for breakfast. Henry and Joe are making pancakes. We need you in the kitchen." There was a loud groan from the other side of the door.

Daphne did the best she could. She needed to have a shower, get the eye drops in her eyes, and at least, brush her hair and slap on a little makeup. She also needed to take a couple of Advil's and spray her mouth with Binaca. By the time she made it to the kitchen, they were clearing the plates. Her plate was sitting there with three pancakes neatly stacked. Henry and Joe had made them. She would have to eat them. The thought made her queasy, but self-hatred for not having been there to watch the making of them was the overriding feeling.

"Good morning, everyone! Sorry to be so slow this morning. Think I'm getting the flu, but the pancakes look delicious! Did you guys really make them?" Daphne's voice sounded firm and cheerful.

"Richard and Magpie helped a little," Joe admitted.

"Pass the maple syrup! I'm not missing out on these!" said Daphne, smiling brightly. She could hear the pounding in her temples and feel the dryness in her eyes. "Since this is such a special occasion having Magpie here, I'm going to celebrate by having a Coke with my pancakes. Will someone bring me a Coke? I want the real thing, no diet drink for me today!" She gulped it down and felt stable enough to get through the pancakes, but it was going to be a long day.

Maggie was glad she made it back to Chicago without any major delays at the airports. The city was covered in snow and she found herself sitting on the sofa most nights not wanting to admit how much she loved the occasional calls she got from Richard. She never mentioned these calls to Daphne despite their daily conversations. That made her a little uneasy, as if she were betraying their friendship by not discussing them in detail, but what was there to say except that Richard would call at random times and say just the thing to make her laugh but never talked for long. He never asked when she was coming to New York. He never reported on the Hones or said what he was doing. Maggie was not sure where she stood with him or where he stood with her.

By February the, calls from Daphne had fallen off and those from Richard became more frequent. Maggie decided to find out what was going on.

"Daphne, I know you're seeing someone and not telling me. Why do I get the answering service half the time when I call?"

"Well, I've had dinner a few times with Alfred Malley."

"Al Malley! You've *got* to be kidding me."

"I know, I know. People don't like him, but that's because no one really knows him."

"Plenty of people know him, Daphne."

"Say no more. The Boalt's, the Pilk's and the Swift's have all weighed in on the subject, and Richard said all the worst things he could think of, but don't worry, I'd never be serious about Al. It's just fun going out to dinner with him."

"I hope you're not the one paying every time."

"No, I'm not. And he takes me to nice places. We went to Gino's last night and Elaine's on Thursday followed by Studio 54. And he's really funny, you know."

"Yes, but his jokes are always at someone else's expense. I'll grant you, he's a skilled mimic, but you be careful. He's a totally bogus guy. "

"Why, Maggie, you sound jealous." Daphne giggled as she sipped her white wine.

"Right. I'd like to give him a piece of my mind. The nerve of him asking you out. And you, going. I should move back to New York and straighten things out. But tell me, how's Studio these days?"

"Not the same, but still fun."

"Oh my God. I can remember some wild nights there."

"Too wild. I don't know how we lived through it."

"You sound like an old woman, Daphne."

"Not at all. Just some of the things we did were dangerous."

"Yeah. I remember some nights I wouldn't want to repeat."

In early March, Maggie was invited to a dinner party at a colleague's house in the Chicago suburbs. One of her friends at the bank, Jake, had a car and offered to drive Maggie and three others out to Winnetka. As they pulled up to the Tudor-style house, the party was already in full swing.

Maggie had two stiff vodkas before they sat down for dinner. She had not had much to drink in the past couple of months and felt the liquor go straight to her head. Her hostess's brother was seated on her left, and as the evening wore on, she noticed him becoming funnier, more intelligent, more handsome. As the candles guttered, he excused himself and went upstairs. In her drunken haze, Maggie imagined he could be The One, followed him up and sat on a bed waiting for him to come out. She smoothed her hair, pinched her cheeks and composed herself in 1950s sex-bomb position leaning back on her elbows with her shapely legs carefully crossed and extended in front of her. When her quarry opened the door he looked at her long and hard, then giving her a lopsided smirk, he said, "Thanks for the offer, but I'm not interested." Ouch. Maggie was not drunk enough.

Downstairs, cocaine was on the table. Maggie declined and went to the bar. Smiling sadly, she poured Vodka over two bedraggled ice cubes. It had been her intention to drink moderately tonight. But after any sort of rejection, a large Vodka was always prescribed, wasn't it? Ever since a bad trip on LSD a decade before gave her a dislike of drugs, she'd stuck to Vodka, drinking wine only at dinner parties.

By the end of the evening everyone was drunk. Jake said he was too drunk to walk, and they would have to decide among them who was the most capable of driving his car back. Maggie was voted most sober and took the compliment in stride. They got to the city with virtually no traffic, and even the Chicago streets were fairly empty. She was beginning to feel tired, a bit drunk and tired. She kept close to the centerline to better see the way, occasionally closing one eye, driving slowly and carefully. Jake was in the passenger seat giving directions and waking up the backseat revelers at their stops. Last one out and now the garage. Maggie's eyes grew wide at the sight of red lights flashing behind her. It happened fast, and Jake left her to organize the bail.

The Cook County jail allowed only one phone call, and she didn't have a home number for Sid Weiss. Calling Daphne, she got the answering service. She recounted her predicament and counted on them to get a detailed message to Daphne as soon as possible. She knew Daphne would then wake up her Uncle Ludlow, and he would find Sid Weiss's emergency number somehow, and Jake would be back soon to post bail. Her confidence wavered when all her belongings were taken away.

The door to the holding cell was locked behind her. She heard it click before the fright set in, adrenalin flooding her bloodstream. Then the panic, the panic. She wasn't prepared for the panic. She sucked air in through her mouth, panting, literally panting. She looked around wild-eyed.

There were six other women in the holding cell, two slumped on plain wooden benches, one sitting on the floor. Three hard-faced girls were leaning against the corner wall, one of them hissed at her, or was she imagining it? Maggie felt her heart pounding hard and sensed the blood leaving her brain. Lightheaded, she stumbled, pitching toward the door. A policewoman approached to release the three women. Someone had posted bail for them.

Maggie was sober now, but it was impossible to think. With great difficulty, she managed to angle her body into the corner just vacated. The remaining three women stared at her, but without menace. Back against the wall, Maggie looked down at her clothes. The glittering backless halter dress Daphne had given her was four inches above her knees, outlandish for the occasion. Traces of perfume and makeup still clung to her. Slowly she slid down to the floor, keeping her knees close to her chest. Exhaustion claimed her consciousness.

Maggie jerked awake. The shift had changed. Coffee was passed around. She overheard one of her cellmates complaining she hadn't had a completed call. "I didn't have a completed call, either, Officer," Maggie said and wondered what had happened to Jake.

"All right, you two. Come with me." The policewoman looked fed up.

Someone put a plastic box in front of Maggie. She found Jake's number among her things; a policeman dialed for her and handed her the receiver. Jake answered on the sixth ring. "Oh, God, Maggie. I've got the cash. But I must've passed out. Give me a few minutes. I'll be right there."

Conscious of her skimpy clothing, Maggie asked the desk sergeant if she could have her shawl back. The request was declined, and she was returned to the cell.

Jake was the classic good guy, much like her father, Maggie thought. She relaxed a little knowing he would be there soon.

Back in the cell, she found a spot to sit down and tried to think without daring to contemplate the long-range repercussions. Just dealing with thoughts of what could happen today was more than enough to keep her off balance. Sipping the lukewarm coffee, she noticed a thin run in her sheer black stockings peeking out from her sequined spikes. She hoped her parents would never find out their daughter had gotten herself in this situation. They were such perfectly straight arrows. Her eyes stung. She loved her parents. They had done their best for her. And here she was having her morning coffee in the Cook County jail. The shame was hotter than the coffee.

Jake paid her bail, took her home in a taxi and convinced her that any good lawyer would be able to keep her name out of the Police Blotter. He went straight to the kitchen, insisting on cooking breakfast while Maggie tracked down Sid Weiss. There had been no message from Daphne. Could she be away for the weekend with Al? Maggie got Ludlow Fowler's number in Oyster Bay from information and reluctantly made the call. It was not easy admitting she needed Sid Weiss on a Sunday morning, but he was unfazed and had the number at hand. God bless lawyers like Ludlow, she thought. They're prepared for anything.

Weiss said he probably could take care of this for her, but pointed out it had only been a few months since her last DUI. And this time, driving without a license. It's so unfair, she thought. Everyone my age drinks as much or more than I do, and I don't even take drugs. I just got caught, that's all. Could have happened to every one of those people at the party. Could have happened to every person I know. Maggie was feeling pretty sorry for herself when Jake said breakfast was ready.

"What'd your lawyer say?"

"He said he probably could keep my name out of the paper."

"It wouldn't go down well at the bank to have it in a second time."

"Do you think they'd fire me?"

"Maybe, maybe not. Best not test the water."

Maggie gave Jake a check for $1000 to cover the bail, and he left to deal with his car and sleep off his hangover. Maggie was depressed and tired, worrying about her career. She had saved nothing and wondered if the banking industry would be closed to her if she were fired. She drank four Cokes and smoked a pack of Marlboro Lights, but that did nothing to dispel the anxiety. Later that evening she thought a beer would make her feel better. Normally, she didn't drink beer and had none in the apartment. Pulling on a pair of jeans and a pale grey sweatshirt, she walked out into the early spring evening. The setting sun flickered through the branches and cast long shadows on the tree trunks. She breathed in the cool, new air. The promise of renewal was all around her, in the pale greening of the leaves to the fresh-faced children laughing on the sidewalks.

She turned into the Seven-Eleven, nodded to the man behind the cash register and went back to the coolers. Pulling an ice-cold 6-pack of Budweiser from the shelf, Daphne turned and saw Jake coming in the door. Blood rushed to her face. How could she be thinking of more drinking after last night? Jake started his wide grin. "Maggie, what a good idea."

"I'm thirsty and thought this would take the curse off the day. Do you want to come back to my place and have a couple of these?"

"Can't. I have a client coming in early tomorrow. I'm just here for some carbs. Man, I'm whipped."

Maggie could feel her face getting hot again. She didn't want her drinking to be anything more than anyone else's. "See you in the morning, Jake, and thanks again for taking such good care of me today."

"Don't mention it. I feel bad that I left you in that cell for five hours. Apologies. You were only driving because the rest of us were in worse shape."

Maggie was relieved to see that Jake didn't seem to remember that bit about her driving without a license. When Maggie walked into her apartment the phone was ringing. She picked up in the kitchen. It was Daphne.

"Maggie, my God, are you alright?"

"I'm okay now, but last night was pretty rough. I'll have to go back to court again in a month."

"How's that going to go down at the bank?"

"Sid thinks he can keep my name out of the paper. They'll never know."

"How did you end up behind the wheel?" Daphne could hear the whoosh of air coming out of the Budweiser bottle and the sound of the cap skidding along the tile counter. "What's that noise?"

"I just opened a real Coke, in a bottle." Maggie thought, I'm lying about my drinking now. "I was the least impaired of the group, so the driving fell to me. And where were you this whole time?"

"I went skiing with Al in Vermont."

Maggie took a long drink of the beer followed by another. Her mouth hydrated, she quaffed two more gulps, and the beer was almost gone. Lighting a cigarette, she drew the smoke deep into her lungs. "Ahhh", she almost said aloud.

"Well, aren't you going to tell me I shouldn't leave the boys to go skiing with a man you don't approve of?" Daphne was tired and not looking forward to a lecture.

"No. You're an adult. You know what I think. I'm not going to go on and on about Al."

"Thank God. You know, none of our friends include me any more. We mainly see Al's friends."

"Who on earth are Al's friends?"

"Now, Maggie, I thought you weren't going to comment."

"I'm just curious." Maggie held her hand over the receiver as she carefully opened the second beer. She felt the tension spill out of her stressed body onto the checkered kitchen floor as she put the bottle to her lips. Smiling, she closed her eyes and let the sound of Daphne's voice soothe her mind while the alcohol caressed her frayed nerves. She was beginning not to care about jail. She would feel fine tomorrow, and next time would be different.

Chapter 7

Maggie smoked and drank and worried for the rest of the month of March. She watched the Chicago River turn emerald green on St. Patrick's Day, preferring to believe the leprechauns made the magic rather than the technical explanation in the *Chicago Sun-Times.* She listened as Daphne talked more and more about Al. She talked to Richard about the growing fear of losing her career. Sid Weiss had, in fact, been able to keep her name out of the paper, and she was pretty sure she could count on Jake's discretion about the night in jail; after all, she was only driving because he was in worse shape than she was, but still, she was on slippery ground.

Walking Maggie into the courthouse one Friday afternoon in early April, Sid leaned over and whispered, "You ready for Judge Marsha Allen?"

Judge Allen was visibly unhappy to see Maggie back in her courtroom so soon. Having no tolerance for repeat offenders, she scowled in her black robes, looking disgusted. Maggie's sentence was thirty hours of community service, thirty AA meetings, a full course of driving school, driver's license revoked for two years and two years of probation.

"If you complete the meetings and community service in sixty days, the record will be expunged at the end of the two-year probation, and you will be allowed to re-apply for a license then." Sid explained after the judge had left the courtroom.

"Just how am I supposed to work my normal fifty hour week, go to driving school, do thirty hours of community service and thirty AA meetings in two months?" Maggie asked Sid as they walked down the marble steps of the courthouse. She could hear the whine in her voice and consciously toned it down.

"Look, Maggie. You've got to do it, or this thing is permanently on your record. Not good for job hunting. Not good for husband hunting. Not good for anything I can think of right now."

"I know. I know. So where's the community service?"

"There're a lot of places, but I usually suggest the soup kitchen at St. Vincent's - they do Sunday lunch. You can go to that driving school on Saturdays. It's only three half-days. And you go to AA on your lunch hour. There's a nooner right near your bank. You're going to get through this."

"Sounds like you know this routine."

"You're not the first person I know with a DUI."

"How about two DUI's in less than six months?" Maggie looked down at her hands.

"You might want to listen at those AA meetings, Maggie. You get someone at St. Vincent's to sign for your hours there. You can do five hours every Sunday. And get signatures at AA You'll be busy, but let me tell you, you don't want a permanent record."

"I know. It would kill my parents. I'll keep in touch, Sid."

"You're not a bad kid, Maggie. Just lay off the booze for a while. Control it, or it'll control you."

They said goodbye on the sidewalk in front of the impressive courthouse, and Sid turned right to walk back to his office. Even though the traffic was heavy on South California Avenue, there were no available taxis. Maggie waited for a good half an hour before a yellow cab stopped to pick her up.

Maggie resolved to start on Sunday at St. Vincent's and check out AA on Monday, but that night she would stir up a pitcher of

Bloody Mary's and talk on the phone; the judge had said nothing about drinking at home.

Maggie went directly to the kitchen, checked the Vodka supply and was happy to see there was plenty of back up. Taking the pitcher, a sixteen-ounce glass and an ice bucket into the living room, she sank into the sofa and called Daphne.

"Maggie! Sorry, but I'm out the door. Tell me quickly what happened at court."

Maggie lit a cigarette, kicked off her navy pumps and put her feet up on the coffee table. "Not so bad. I'm going to work in a soup kitchen at one of the Catholic churches, take a driving class and attend a few AA meetings. No license for a couple of years, but, hey, it could've been worse."

"You'll like the soup kitchen. But AA Meetings? What for? You're not an alcoholic."

"I know. It's weird, and I have to have this paper signed every time I go. Proof for the judge that I was there. Thirty signatures."

"Oh my God, Maggie! I want to hear more, but I've got to go. Call you tomorrow."

Maggie looked at her watch. Six o'clock in Chicago. Seven in New York. Maybe Richard was still in his office. She called, but the phone just rang and rang. She'd never called his home number before.

She called her parents. She got the answering service and chatted with them for a few minutes, then switched on the TV. Nothing worth watching.

She called Gino's for pizza. Before it arrived, Maggie had finished the Bloody Mary's. Feeling cheerful and confident, she made a second pitcher, this time with Vodka and grapefruit juice, and thought, 'I've made it through. Neither the Bank nor my parents need ever know about this. I can stay out of driving situations - easy. I'll love the soup kitchen and make that something I do every Sunday, even bringing friends to help. I'll be an inspiration to many.' The image of a rose-colored future warmed her heart with expansive, optimistic plans.

The pizza arrived and Maggie thought how cute the delivery-man was. He was probably a struggling actor or writer or something. Maybe. But no time to get to know him, not now with all this extra work.

She looked at her watch. Nine-thirty. She checked to see if Daphne was home. Not yet. She got out her address book and looked at Richard's home number. Just looking, she thought. She closed her eyes for a few minutes. When she opened them again it was ten fifteen in Chicago. Eleven fifteen in New York. She called Richard's home number.

His sleepy voice answered. Softly, she said, "Richard, it's Maggie."

"Maggie, it's late."

"My court appearance was today."

"Tell me about it." He suddenly sounded alert and interested.

"The judge has something against drinking. I have to go to thirty AA meetings, among other things, but I won't have a permanent record, if I do it by the book."

"Have you been drinking tonight, Maggie?"

"No, I'm just tired and need some sympathy." Maggie vaguely noticed the lie.

"I'll give you all the sympathy you want, but make sure you don't end up with a criminal record. I don't mean to sound dramatic, but it would ruin your career."

Maggie wanted him to tell her she shouldn't worry. She wanted him to tell her this happened to everyone and that the judge was over-reacting. She wanted to hear him say, "You drink normally, just like everyone else your age. "

"But, I mean, really, *AA?*"

"It's not so bad. I have a college roommate who's been going to those meetings for a couple of years. He's one of the best men I know. And you've *got* to take this thing seriously, Maggie."

She could feel her face getting hot. Who was he to shame her? Get off the phone and forget about him. Too old, obviously. Eight years older. He just doesn't get how things are now.

"I've got to go, Richard. You have a nice weekend." Maggie hung up, reached for some ice cubes to refresh her drink and swaddled herself in Vodka and self-pity.

Maggie's consciousness swam back to the surface on Saturday around noon. For a moment she wondered where she was. In her own bed, in her apartment at 1400 Lakeshore Drive in Chicago. Of course. But not a good sign to feel dizzy while still horizontal. She would not open her eyes just yet. One by one her nerve endings started checking in.

After twenty minutes, Maggie accepted that every cell in her frontal cortex was in acute pain. In order to avoid active nausea she would have to remain completely still and hope her stomach would adjust. It didn't, though, and a dash to the john got her to her knees just in time to loose a gallon of toxic waste. Slowly she got to her feet and staggered to the sink. Squeezing a lot of blue toothpaste onto her toothbrush took most of her available energy, but she managed to force the toothbrush under cold water and circle it around her mouth. She raised her aching head and saw her reflection in the mirror above the sink. She wet a washcloth and wiped her face. Her cheeks were puffy. Her eyes were reduced to flaming slits. She turned away and crawled back under the covers.

At three o'clock the phone next to her bed exploded. The noise was shocking. It was insulting how it wouldn't give up. Finally, she could hear the whir of the tape and her own chirpy voice announcing she was not home and encouraging the caller to leave a message after the beep. It was intolerable. She listened resentfully as Daphne's voice filled the room. Daphne hoped that Maggie had slept well and that Maggie would call her later. 'Not today', Maggie thought. 'I've just got to get through without talking or being talked at.' Maggie hoped there was a cold beer in the refrigerator and a box of instant mashed potatoes in the cupboard. If she could have some mashed potatoes and a very cold beer, maybe she could face what was left of the day.

There was no beer. Nor any mashed potatoes. Maggie swigged some Coke out of a giant plastic bottle and burped. Gross, she thought but didn't care. The smell of last night's pizza was revolting and sent her back to the john, then back to bed. Never again, she thought as she drifted down into delta waves.

By six o'clock she finally felt stable. She thought she would call her colleague and neighbor and see if he were free.

"Jake, it's Maggie. I had my court date yesterday."

"How'd it go?"

"Fine. First offence and all." Maggie hardly even noticed the lie. "I feel a little down and was wondering if you want to go out for a hamburger or something."

"Yeah. That'd be great. I'll come by your place and in about an hour. We can walk over to Arnie's. I'll make the reservation."

Maggie felt revived enough to get rid of the pizza box, wash the pitcher, have a shower and dress for dinner. No more Vodka, ever.

On Sunday morning Maggie was only slightly hung over from Arnie's house red wine. She managed to check in at St. Vincent's soup kitchen by nine-thirty where her first job was to mop the floor and then get started on the sandwiches. It was a long five hours, but she felt she'd at least been useful.

"Thanks, Maggie. Great job. Hope you'll come next Sunday." The soup kitchen captain was pleased.

"I'll be here at nine o'clock sharp." Maggie smiled. "Thanks for signing my community hours sheet. I look forward to next Sunday."

That evening, Maggie heated up some Campbell's Cream of Celery soup. She put just a little bit of sherry in it, not enough to count, and decided not to have a drink. Feeling virtuous but lonely, she called Daphne.

"Daphne, are you sitting down?" Without waiting for a reply, Maggie continued, "I just want to tell you, I thought of you because I loved working in the soup kitchen. The guests were great, and I met some nice volunteers. Really interesting people. One of the women is the voice of a couple of the Disney cartoon characters."

"Cool job. And I'm not surprised you liked it. As you know, volunteering at St. James' on Tuesdays is a big part of my life. Will you go everyday?"

"Just once a week, on Sunday. I have a job, remember? They have a piano in the parish hall and a man who plays for the Chicago Philharmonic played and sang during lunch. He comes most Sundays."

"Are any of the others there for community service?"

"I don't think so, but I'm not sure. I think the others are regular volunteers. The captain didn't make a big deal about signing my papers. I doubt the others even noticed. But if they did, I wouldn't care. They don't seem like judgmental types."

"I'm sure they aren't. I really like the people I work with. Bet you end up doing this after your sentence is over."

"I was sentenced to thirty hours, so six weeks of Sundays like today, but I think you're right. I've spent many worse Sundays, believe me."

"I do believe you because I've spent them with you. Listening to a great pianist while feeding the hungry sounds good to me. Guess what. I have some good news."

"Tell me."

"Louisa has a boyfriend."

"Oh, my God. I'm so glad. Every time I think of Kenny Lang my blood boils. What's the boyfriend like?"

"He's an American over there on a Rhodes scholarship."

"Just right. Please give her my love when you talk to her."

"I will. Johnny's in town, and I'll see him tomorrow so I'll find out more."

"And I'll be spending my lunch hour at AA"

"How does that work? Do you bring a sandwich or what?"

"I have no idea, but I'll let you know tomorrow." Maggie was careful not to mention calling Richard to Daphne. She couldn't believe she'd called him so late and was mortified that she'd hung up on him. Realizing how much she looked forward to hearing from him and hoping this wouldn't end his phone calls, she felt shimmer of shame about her drunkenness.

Monday mornings were always busy at the bank, and by the time Maggie got to the AA meeting, the room was crowded. Slipping into a seat in the back row, she was surprised to find a room of mainly well-dressed professionals. Self-consciously, she looked around and noticed the woman in charge of produce at the local A&P was sitting in her row. They nodded to each other. As she continued to look around, her eyes stopped dead on the meeting leader. Air came in sharply through her nose; she dared not exhale. It was Sean O'Reilly, the senior vice-president and manager of her bank. *He's here to fire me. That bitch of a judge told him, and he's here to catch me and fire me. I've got to get out of here.* The door was closed, and the room was quiet as the meeting began. Leaving at this point was out of the question; all eyes would be on her. Maggie shrank down in her seat.

"Hi, I'm Sean," her boss said, "and I'm an alcoholic." "Hi, Sean," the room answered.

Maggie's heart was beating fast. What kind of joke was this? The sound of her own shallow breathing filled her ears; her whole being was fixated on the door waiting for an opportunity to escape. Could she create a diversion and slink out? No. She was a prisoner here just as surely as being locked up in that cell.

Maggie was aware of different people speaking, but her attention did not waver, focusing on the door with her mind and her eyes. Other people came in and out of the door, but she would be the one O'Reilly would see. She was the one he came to fire. Then, suddenly everyone was standing up, but several people blocked the door. *Oh, my God. They're not going to hold hands, are they?* The woman from the A&P took her hand, and she became part of a circle with her boss starting a prayer. *This is the living end.* Maggie looked at the floor.

The next thing she knew, Sean O'Reilly was by her side. "Hello, Maggie. Great to see you here. You know, a mean judge sentenced me to AA meetings seventeen years ago, and it was the best thing that ever happened to me. I see you have a paper to be signed, I'd be happy to sign it for you." Sean obviously remembered seeing her name in the Police Blotter.

"Mr. O'Reilly, I'm so embarrassed." Maggie blurted out.

"Call me Sean, and don't be embarrassed. We're all here for the same reason. You're in a safe place, Maggie."

A safe place, my foot. This is a crazy nightmare, she thought as she turned over her court paper to be signed. While signing, Sean said, "I'd like to introduce you to some of the women who'll be able to help you."

Help me! They're alcoholics. What's wrong with this man? "I have to get back to the bank."

"Not yet. Della, come meet my friend Maggie." Sean called to a beautiful brunette dressed in skinny jeans tucked into long choc- olate-colored boots folded over under the knee, pirate-style, and a fleece-lined bomber jacket.

Della gave Maggie her home and office numbers, and said, "I come to this meeting several times a week. Call me any time. We can have coffee after the meeting. I'd love to tell you my story."

Maggie mumbled and bolted out of the room. She didn't want to hear anybody's story, for goodness sake. She just wanted no per- manent record. What was this woman thinking about? On the street, she realized she was sweating under her trench coat in the cold, damp April afternoon. She went to the bar at the Palmer House Hotel. She sat at a table, ordered a Bloody Mary and a chicken sandwich. She asked the waiter to have a phone brought to the table and called Daphne at work, hoping that Richard would not answer, not that he ever had, but this was not her day.

"Thank God you're there, Daphne. I feel like I'm in the twilight zone."

"What's going on?"

"I went to that AA meeting and who's there leading the thing but my boss, one of the most important bankers in the Midwest. Can you beat that? He was friendly enough after the meeting and introduced me to this woman who wants me to call her so she can tell me about herself. Can you imagine? Maybe I could help her out sometime, but not *now* with all I have to do."

"What went on in the meeting? I'm so curious."

"A bunch of different people talked about nothing in particular. I didn't really pay that much attention. I was just trying to figure out why Mr. O'Reilly was there. Afterwards he told me a mean judge had sent him."

"He must be an alcoholic. Stay clear of him. He'll want you to join the cult. Al says it's a cult."

"You didn't tell Al that I'm going to AA, did you? Please tell me you are not sharing my private life with him."

"Just in general. We were talking about AA in general."

"Daphne, that's a big fat lie. Nobody talks about AA in general. You've told him everything, haven't you? It won't be a nanosecond until all of New York knows. I can't believe you did this to me." Maggie could feel the bile rising slowly from her lower abdomen to her throat. Her anger was in her mouth, but she washed it down with the Bloody Mary and waited for Daphne's reply.

"You know perfectly well Al knows. When you called Friday at midnight you told him yourself. Don't tell me you forgot that."

"No, I didn't forget; I just don't remember mentioning AA to him." Maggie cringed. *How could I have talked to Al Malley about my private life?* Her anger morphed into some new, nameless, dreadful fear.

"Well, you did. You were just so tired, you don't remember. You sounded half asleep. You've been working too hard, and you've been too worried about this DUI business, Maggie. Why don't you take a Valium and get some rest tonight? Call me when you get home."

SLIDING

Walking back to work, Maggie thought about what Daphne had said and felt a frisson of panic not remembering the midnight call. *But it's true. I'm very tired. Too tired to remember right now. Maybe I should see a doctor and get myself a prescription for Valium. Just enough to get me through.*

Chapter 8

Every spring a small dinner dance in held at Old Westbury Gardens for patrons of this botanical treasure. It is the one event that *le tout Long Island* attends. Old guard mixes with new residents to raise money for continuing the perfection. Ludlow invited Daphne for the weekend with the boys and their nanny, Marie. He always subscribed and took a table of eight, this year inviting Mayor Koch, New York's premiere bachelor, Arabella Yamada and his neighbors on both sides of his house in Oyster Bay.

On the night of the dance, Ludlow had Fred pick up Arabella at the Sherry Netherlands and bring her to his house so he could escort both Daphne and Arabella. Ludlow and Arabella had several friends in common, and he was sure she would enjoy herself at this dance. Torches illuminated the winding drive, and the huge tent glowed orange on the east side of the mansion in the late spring twilight.

They arrived on the early side so that Ludlow would be there to greet the rest of his guests. The presence of the brash and controversial mayor would be unusual in this mostly conservative gathering, and Ludlow wanted to smooth the way.

Arabella, petite and erect in a dark blue square-necked Oscar de la Renta, looked regal in her amazing parure of turquoise and diamond jewelry. Years ago, Yoshi had seen it in the window of Van Cleef and Arpels on Fifty-seventh and Fifth. Thinking the turquoise would complement Arabella's startling blue eyes, he went right in and bought the whole thing - necklace, earrings, bracelets and ring. Arabella did not have many occasions to wear these, but she wore them whenever possible to honor her adored Yoshi. Daphne was a knockout in a pale apple green organza studded with orange silk poppies. Dusting off her mother's diamonds, she wore an impressive bracelet and earrings.

Ronaldo Maia himself did the flowers, and Glorious Food was the caterer. No dinner in America could have been more stylish that night. Every detail was perfect, and all the wine glasses were constantly topped up by white-gloved waiters. Daphne was having a good time chatting with the Mayor and somehow lost count of the glasses. The Mayor had become Ed by the time dessert arrived, and while dancing with him, she slipped and fell heavily onto the short, wiry man. He broke her fall, laughing, but both of them were shaken and returned to the table before anything else happened.

That Wednesday Maggie called Daphne at the office. "Have you seen Page Six?" She was referring to the social gossip page in the New York Post.

"No. Something interesting?"

"The dance at Old Westbury Gardens. You didn't tell me you were 'unsteady'."

"What? Read it to me."

"It says. 'Whoops, was the beautiful Daphne Hone over-served? She seemed rather unsteady on the dance floor with our favorite Mayor.'"

"Oh, crap. I can't believe it. That was one slippery dance floor, and I just slipped a little. That's all. Why on earth would someone bother to write about that? Who cares if I slipped? Who cares if I drink Champagne at a party? These people should find something worthwhile to write about."

"Don't worry. Everyone who reads it today will forget it tomorrow."

"What else does it say?" asked Daphne, worried about what she might have forgotten.

"Oh, it says Arabella looked chic and danced with your Uncle Ludlow and the Mayor. It says Mayor Koch knew many of the assembled Long Islanders and that it was the most beautiful party of the season. According to Page Six, there has never been such a tent – all lined in apricot silk. Blah, blah, blah. Sounds like quite some party."

"Yes. It was flawless. Except for the dance floor. I've got to go. Call you later." Daphne wondered how many people she'd have to call. What would she say? The heel fell off her shoe? She twisted her ankle? Or she could deride the Mayor's dancing, saying she's sure everyone dancing with him was 'unsteady' since he has two left feet.

Maggie continued to go to the lunchtime meetings of AA Sometimes Sean O'Reilly was there and sometimes not. He was always friendly and introduced her to many of the women. They all gave Maggie their phone numbers and told her to call, which of course, she never would. Most nights she drank on the phone with Daphne, but she consciously made an effort to cut back. Sometimes this was successful and sometimes not. And she looked forward to Sundays. She loved working at the soup kitchen and got through driving school with flying colors. Everything was going well, and May brought the most glorious weather. She had fifteen signatures from AA and had started listening at the meetings and even laughing at the stories people told. The level of honesty was refreshing. She thought of calling Della. Why not go out with her after work one day?

"Look at you, Maggie, you've barely had anything to drink in the last three weeks. Look at how other people drink! You *never* drink in the morning. And you hardly ever drink during the day, do you?" Daphne was insisting that Maggie was not an alcoholic.

"Hardly ever. And many of the AA people say they drank for thirty years or more. They're the real alcoholics, not us. But I have to keep going for the signatures. Judge Marsha Allen, remember?"

"Right, but you be careful. They're sneaky and want you to join them. Al says it's dangerous."

Maggie laughed. "Al wouldn't think that if he could see these people. They're a pretty safe lot."

"But it's a cult."

"What nonsense. A cult needs a leader, and a cult is easy to get into and hard to get out of. AA has no leader, no rules. And no trouble getting out, that's for sure."

"Al says you should go as little as possible."

"What the hell does Al know about AA? Nothing, I bet. Anyway, not from personal experience."

"Now, Magpie, you sound a little out of sorts."

"Sorry, Daphne. I know you like him, and I do, too. It's just my enthusiasm for him is more restrained."

The next day, Maggie went to the meeting determined to find something interesting to tell Daphne about afterwards. One man described himself as an ego-manic with an inferiority complex. She couldn't wait to tell Daphne.

Della came up to her after the meeting. "Maggie, do you have time for a quick bite?"

Maggie was surprised to hear herself say, "I'd like that."

The two women sat across from each other in a booth at the corner coffee shop. "I get the picture that you work with Sean at the bank," Della commented.

Maggie was startled hearing Della call her boss Sean and knowing where he worked. "Actually, I work *for* Mr. O'Reilly. He's the big boss."

"Yeah, I know. My father used to work with him at the Northern Trust before Sean made the move to your bank."

"What do you do, Della?"

"Fashion writer for the *Sun-Times*. I've been with them for the last year."

"What did you do before that?"

"I had my own business. Started painting tote bags when I was seventeen, and somehow ended up with a whole accessory line. You know purses, shawls, and all that sort of thing. I had a bit of luck, and my style caught on. Then when I was twenty-two, there were these other designers I worked with and we started partying. Cocaine got a hold of me fast, and by thirty, I was bankrupt in every way. It stole everything from me – my creativity, my business, my integrity."

Della's far-away look disappeared. She looked Maggie in the eye. "I lived in that nightmare for a few years, until finally I couldn't go on anymore and tried to take myself out with pills. The E. R. doctor who pumped my stomach knew a lot about addiction and made sure I had counseling. The up-shot is, I've been clean and sober for two years, and now I have this wonderful job with the *Sun-Times*."

"I'm sorry you went through all that. I'm so lucky I never liked drugs."

"I've seen alcohol take a lot of people down."

"But I'm not an alcoholic. My mother might be, but I don't think I am."

'It's a self-diagnosed disease, Maggie." Della looked down at her watch. "Look at the time! I've got to get back to work. But about my drinking – I found I just couldn't drink responsibly anymore."

"What do you mean 'drink responsibly'?"

"Oh, you know, I could decide not to have much to drink one night, and that would be fine. Then next time I'd decide that, I'd end up wasted. I just never knew what would happen. You've got my number. Give me a call. I'd love to see you again."

Maggie stayed to finish her coffee. She looked out the window noticing the light change and rain begin to fall. She watched a mother gather her two children under a red umbrella, cross the street and come into the coffee shop, shrugging off the rain. They sat in the booth across from her and ordered French toast with hot chocolate.

Maggie took the last sip from her cup, thinking about what Della had said. She could certainly relate to not knowing where the drink would lead.

She thought of her father and remembered him walking her to school one day, her little hand in his big one. She was wearing the green uniform dress and brown oxfords, neatly tied. Walking up East End Avenue, he said to her, "Maggie, always remember when you close your mind, you lock more out than you lock in." She had often thought of that piece of wisdom and could hear his voice across all those years.

Chapter 9

Daphne knew she was under Al's spell. He was good-looking and not without charm. Her old friends openly disliked him, and even she was beginning to see his similarity to Kenny. But her lust for him was at the point that just hearing the sound of his voice on the phone made her ache for him.

All was going well, until one Monday evening in mid-May. After dinner in Daphne's garden, candlelight reflecting off four empty bottles of wine, Al suggested ending the evening with a bottle of Champagne.

Swaying slightly as she stood up, Daphne held on to the table to steady herself. "I think you've had enough."

Al shoved the table as he staggered to his feet, a crystal glass shattered on the flagstones. He turned to face her. "What do you mean I've had enough? You're the lush. You're nothing but a lush." He grabbed her upper arms roughly and glared down at her.

With drunken bravado Daphne spat out, "So you think I'm a lush, do you? There's not one decent person in New York City who has any respect for you. You're well known for exactly what you are. A good for nothing moocher."

Still gripping one of her arms, Al slapped her with the back of his other hand, knuckles digging into her cheek. Daphne's knees buckled, but she managed to catch her balance. "Get out of here, you bastard, and don't you ever come back." Daphne tightened her lips and narrowed her green eyes.

Straightening himself to his full height, muscles tightening in a physical effort to regain some dignity, Al turned to leave quietly, looking over his shoulder. "You look sexy," he slurred and left.

Daphne stood there in the dark garden watching him leave, swinging between outrage and desire.

Later, brushing her teeth, she got a look at herself in the mirror and was surprised to see a mark. After all, the slap had been nearly painless. She thought the mark would diffuse over night, and nothing would ever need to be said about the incident.

In the morning the bruises were prominent, on her face and her arms, but her anger had died. Al was drunk and didn't mean what he'd said; she'd convinced herself of that. And she didn't mean what she'd said, either. *But what to say about this face?*

Sitting at the breakfast table, she could see that Marie and the boys were waiting for her to say something. Her hand flew to her cheek. "Oh, the bruise! The swinging door to the kitchen hit me when my hands were full." The two women knew this meant silence on the subject. Daphne repeated the lie at the office.

Al did not call her that day or the next. On Thursday flowers arrived on Daphne's desk with a note. "We both said things we didn't mean. How about dinner tonight at Lutece? I'll pick you up at eight. Al." Daphne sat still and thought about this, knowing if she accepted, they would be back together. Did she really want this? Yes and no. But, on the whole, more yes than no. There was no one else in her life right now, and hadn't she and Maggie discussed the dearth of men in New York and Chicago? Maybe it would be better to have Al than no one.

That night she camouflaged the bruises on her cheek with makeup, and the evening was lavish with loving apologies, ending at Al's apartment.

Since things were going well again with Al, for the next few weeks Daphne found less time to talk to Maggie. Anyway, it was not much fun to hear her best friend talking about AA. *Al's right. It's a cult, and they're brainwashing Maggie.* Daphne might have to go out to Chicago again and intervene if things got too extreme.

That Sunday Daphne wondered who there was in her life she could actually talk to and ended by calling Arabella Yamada. Daphne told her about Maggie's DUI's. "She was mandated to AA, and they're trying to convince her she's an alcoholic. Al thinks it's dangerous. And it sounds like they're brainwashing her to me."

"Well, Daphne, personally, I've never seen Maggie drink that much, but then I've only met her a few times. And if she's gotten two DUI's in six months, her brain probably could do with a bit of a wash. It's not okay to drink and drive. She's lucky not to have killed a carload of innocent people, and she definitely shouldn't have a license until she stops driving under the influence."

Daphne was surprised at Arabella's reaction.

"Maggie's not doing anything anyone else's not doing. She was only driving the last time because she was the least impaired of the group."

"That doesn't mean she couldn't have killed someone."

"But you drink!"

"Certainly not while I'm driving."

'Al thinks…"

"Don't tell me what Al thinks. Tell me what *you* think. How would you feel if your boys were maimed or killed by a drunk driver?"

Daphne was silent. She thought how lucky it was that she never had to drive in the city. There was always a taxi or Lionel. Then she thought about Maine. She knew there were times she drove when she shouldn't and promised herself to be more careful.

"Daphne, be proud of Maggie. She's looking at her life and maybe she'll want to make some changes. You know what Socrates said: 'The unexamined life is not worth living.' He was generally right about everything, I've found."

"It's just that I don't think there is anything abnormal about Maggie's drinking."

"I studied a little bit about alcoholism years ago. About half of all Asian people have an allergic reaction to alcohol. Yoshi never drank, but he had a friend who turned bright red if he had even one sip. It is a strange disease and needs to be treated as a disease."

"I doubt Maggie has a disease."

"Well, you would know better than I."

Daphne was restless and irritable for the remainder of the day. She couldn't wait to put the boys to bed and have dinner with Al. She felt betrayed by Arabella. She knew this was irrational and childish, which just made the resentment stronger.

After having a drink and hearing the details of the conversation, Al's only comment was, "She's an old woman. What does she know about life?"

Everything inside of Daphne wanted to defend Arabella and proclaim her wisdom, but she heard herself sigh and say, "You're right, Al. As always. Maggie's taking this whole thing too seriously, but I can't tell her to stop. She needs more signatures for the judge. Don't you think it's strange that a judge would recommend a cult like that?"

"You know people love to exaggerate everything. Don't worry Maggie will come to her senses. Will she be coming to Maine this summer?"

"Of course."

"We can work on her then."

Daphne was surprised that Al already assumed he would be spending the summer with her in Maine. The cottage she rented had only one small guest room. Feeling flattered by the 'we' but irritated by the assumption, she poured another glass of wine. Her thinking seesawed. One moment she thought, 'At least I have Al', and the next thought was, 'Who does he think he is?' As the evening wore on it became, 'I'm so lucky to have Al', and ended on that note.

Springtime changed the mood in Chicago. People were peeling off layers of clothes, smiling at each other and the nannyberry bushes were in blossom. Maggie was close to having the needed thirty signatures but decided she might follow Della's suggestion to try ninety meetings in ninety days while not drinking. She would talk to Della about what the steps meant and see what happened. Just see.

She plucked up the courage and opened up to her mother about the DUI's, swearing her to secrecy, and mentioned she was going to try AA She even suggested her mother find some Alanon meetings to go to so she could find out what it was all about. Maggie couldn't help hoping her mother might come to see that her own binge drinking was unusual and harmful.

Ever since Maggie could remember, every few months her mother would become comatose with drink. Most of the time she was reliable and sweet, but then, without warning she would 'disappear on them'. That's how Maggie and her father described her binges. Selena Miller had grown up in Florida, and Maggie's father thought if she could have a greenhouse for her beloved orchids she would drink less, and he moved the family from New York to Connecticut. The greenhouse provided a nice little business and also a good place to hide bottles. Maggie had always felt responsible for her mother and always kept the drinking secret, even Daphne didn't know about it. Living in Chicago relieved Maggie of this self-imposed burden and hearing stories about binge drinking at AA meetings, Maggie was able to understand her mother's problem and wanted to help her.

Maggie wanted to tell Daphne about her experiment of going to meetings daily for three months, but sensed Daphne would be against it. It meant hiding something else from Daphne, like the phone calls with Richard. Would this jeopardize their friendship?

They had shared everything for so many years. Something didn't feel right.

Later that night Richard called, and Maggie was excited to tell him she was going to commit to ninety days of going to meetings and not drinking. "Good decision. No matter what happens, you'll be wiser for having done this. Remember, I told you I have a good friend in AA? He was in pretty bad shape before he went, and now, well, I don't know anyone I admire more. He has really straightened out his life. His wife had left him, and now they're back together with a baby on the way."

"How long has he been in the program?

"Two or three years now. I'll introduce you to him next time you're here. You'll like him."

"I feel funny about not telling Daphne that I'm doing this, but I know she would discourage me. She thinks A. A. is some kind of cult. Or rather Al tells her it is."

"Al Malley's a fine one to talk. Every time I see that man, he's making an ass out of himself, usually because he's drunk. I don't understand what Daphne sees in him."

"She says he makes her laugh. And you have to admit, he's good-looking."

"I don't have to admit anything of the sort. Al likes to say it's a cult because he makes fun of what he can't understand. You know how he is."

Maggie had a similar conversation with Della over lunch later that same week. She talked about not wanting to tell Daphne about her decision to try AA

"We talk on the phone several times a week, and I feel like I'm lying to her. Won't she notice a difference in me?"

"On the phone?" Della sounded confused.

"Well, we usually drink together on the phone."

"Can't you have a Coke instead?"

"I guess I can. Why not?"

Walking back to work, Maggie thought how dim she must have sounded to Della, but somehow that did not matter. Della would never judge her. She knew that.

Maggie reported to Daphne that the judge had commended her on her prompt compliance with the community service and AA attendance. But of course, there would still be probation for two years.

Daphne seemed to be in a good mood, too. "The man at the Wilson School says things are much better these days. Joe's reading is up to snuff, and Henry's not been cursing, or at least no one has caught him."

"See? I told you. They're stars."

"They're growing so fast, though. I just want to wave my arms and yell 'Stop'." After that there seemed to be little more to say. During this strange silence, Daphne wondered what she could talk about that did not include Al, and Maggie thought about saying she was seeing Della once or twice a week but decided not to. Then finally, Daphne said, "I have the house in Maine from July 15th through Labor Day. When do you want to come?"

"How about Labor Day weekend?"

"I was hoping you'd spend a couple of weeks, as usual."

"Didn't I tell you?" Maggie said. "I'm going to London with Mom. We leave on August 20th for a week. Then a few days in

Connecticut when we get back so Labor Day in Maine would work out perfectly. I've really missed you and the boys."

"We've missed you, too." Putting down the phone, Daphne wondered what she would tell Al about his having to make other plans for Labor Day. She knew him well enough by now to know he'd have some sarcastic remark to make about that.

As it turned out, it was worse than she expected. "So, I just dance to your tune when it suits you? I know how you like to control everything, Daphne. But you have to remember, it's not *all* about you."

This was not the first time Al chose to criticize her. More and more their evenings ended in argument. "The fact is I couldn't care less if Maggie is more important to you. I'll spend Labor Day with the Varley's in Southampton, as always."

"'As always', Al? I thought their house was only finished at the end of last summer."

"Let me be precise, Daphne. I spent last Labor Day there and had a wonderful time. And I'm sure I'll have a wonderful time there this year without you."

"You know I love being with you. But Maggie usually spends a couple of weeks with us, and this summer she's coming only for Labor Day weekend. The boys love her, and she's family to them."

"I just told you. I don't give a damn. I'm *always* welcome at the Varley's."

Chapter 10

As it turned out, bad feelings about Labor Day did not get in the way of a visit to the Varley's just two weeks later. Al was anxious that they meet even though Daphne had been putting it off, turning down invitations for dinner at their duplex apartment in the River House and weekends at their houses in Palm Beach, Aspen and Southampton.

Daphne had heard and read a lot about the Varley's and suspected that Al's admiration for them was more about their triumphant bank balance than their sterling characters. Everyone knew the Varley's spent an immense amount of money on public relations, but even so, people had to admit, mysterious and fascinating as they were, the Varley's were completely devoid of every social grace. She'd heard Chuck Varley resembled cotton candy, all pink and glossy, his long fingers like lobster legs, his thinning coppery hair gelled, blown and swirled with exceptional care, looking like a forty-five year-old boy about to be photographed. In actual fact, the cruel set of his mouth told a different story.

Al and Daphne set out for Southampton in Daphne's old station wagon late Thursday afternoon of the 4th of July weekend. Tiffany Varley was waiting for them at the top of the steps of her Italianate mansion on Meadow Lane, stick thin and perfectly groomed with every streak in her magnificent mane artfully placed by Frederic Fekkai himself and dressed head to toe in Chanel. Daphne had seen her picture so often in various publications that she would have recognized her anywhere.

"Daphne, how wonderful to have you here at last! I can't wait to show you the house. Al must've told you we've only just moved in, so it's not quite as I want it, but let Al take your things and follow me." Al carried the suitcases to a beautiful guest suite on the ground floor next to the library.

Daphne had read that the house was built and decorated by an architect/designer duo from California, totally unknown on the East Coast. It soon became clear they would remain unknown for some time still given the schizophrenic relationship between exterior, interior and site. Daphne was no architect herself, but she recognized style when she saw it. And this wasn't it. Granted, the Italian palazzo with its classical gardens would look comfortable in the Tuscan countryside, but here on the Hampton dunes, it looked bizarre. Inside the house, it was all black leather, white marble and chrome. Lovely old-fashioned roses craned their necks in massive glass cubes, and scented candles overwhelmed the smell of the sea.

Daphne grew up with fourth-generation summer residents of Southampton and was often a houseguest in their weather-beaten shingle cottages. She'd heard that they thought the Varley's were exceptionally vulgar people, even by current Southampton standards, and that their new place was run like a Four Seasons Hotel, complete with complimentary products in the bathrooms and room service menus. She knew her friends would look askance at the Varley's six bay garage supporting the helicopter pad, but she also knew most of them were dying to be invited *chez* Varley to see for themselves.

While Tiffany showed off the house, Daphne watched the bejeweled fingers grab at everything, moving and straightening the many objects. Tiffany even opened the large safe in her dressing room to show Daphne a collection of jewelry, which would have impressed the most indulged Hollywood star. Daphne was staggered by the sheer quantity of clothes and jewels. There must have been six running feet of white blouses alone all lined up, hanging on yellow satin hangers.

After the house tour, Daphne and Tiffany joined Al and Chuck and two other couples on the terrace. Daphne watched as Tiffany pretended indifference while silently observing everything from half-closed eyes, trying to mask her intense interest while registering how each comment related to her, her husband and their goals.

Daphne realized there could never be enough for Tiffany. Not enough success, not enough money, not enough fame, not enough stuff. At some level Tiffany knew this, too, and misery was written all over her gaunt, surgically improved face. The sun was setting, and in the half-light, Daphne could see Tiffany's tiny bright eyes take in, sort and access everything and everyone around her, assigning precise monetary or social values.

During dinner it became obvious that Al was Tiffany's favorite. She loved him for who and what he knew. She loved hearing him gossip about all generations of the old guard with no juicy detail omitted. His intimate knowledge of old Southampton seemed to make her feel deliciously a part of, yet superior to, that group.

"Al, tell the story about your grandfather and old man Cutter." Tiffany wanted the whole table's attention for this.

"Not much of a story, really. My grandfather taught Mr. Cutter to play golf, as he did so many of that generation, and Mr. Cutter wanted him to be his partner at a Member/Guest event in Florida. Of course my grandfather was a professional and sneaking in a professional partner was frowned on in those days. It was considered a social sin in the 60s. Mr. Cutter was even asked to resign from the Jupiter Island Club. He got Mrs. Reed's famous black sweater to make it clear he was never to return." It was a great story for Tiffany. She loved that the Cutters couldn't belong to the Jupiter Island Club anymore. She knew Adele Cutter would never let her and Chuck become members of the nearby beach club so hearing of the father's disgrace made her day.

"And what about your father and the ever mysterious and glamorous Miss Frost?" Tiffany urged Al on.

"Let's just leave it that he improved her golf game substantially, and she taught him a thing or two about art."

For over fifty years either Al's father or his grandfather had taught the Southamptonians how to play beautiful golf on the most challenging course on Long Island. His father and grandfather were loved and respected golf pros, and Al's natural athletic grace was always commented upon whenever his name came up. It was members of the golf club who had banded together and paid for Al's expensive education, and he hated them for it. From his first semester at St. Paul's, he could always be counted on to create opportunities to make fun of them and their way of life. But this particular evening Al did not pursue the subject. Daphne had kicked him under the table. It was time to stop. She was never one for gossip and these stories about old family friends had annoyed her. What was she doing here with these people?

It was late by the time dinner was over and when the other guests left, Daphne went off to bed, leaving Al to have a brandy with Tiffany and Chuck. The Varley's never seemed to get sick of Al's stories and stayed up with him even though neither of them were big drinkers. For some reason Al got on the subject of his years at Columbia University. They always liked hearing about his fraternity, and Al recounted the initiation rites of St. Anthony's Hall. The Varley's hung on his every word.

The next morning Daphne got up early for a walk on the beach, but Al was at the breakfast table trying to make amends, "Look, Chuck, I don't know what got into me last night. Please don't mention what I told you about St. A.'s. It's stupid stuff, but it's supposed to be secret."

"Don't worry. I don't know anyone interested in college pranks, but you might tell Tiffany. She was already talking about it this morning on the phone with her sister."

All those years Al had kept the secret. Many nights he had been far drunker than last night. What had made him bring it up to these people, of all people?

A few moments later Tiffany came into the breakfast room. "Tiffany! Good morning!" Al sounded hardier than he felt. "I'm embarrassed that I bored you with all that college nonsense last night."

"I wasn't bored at all. I thought it was riveting."

"Chuck said you mentioned it to Shirley. Please ask her not to pass it on."

"Oh, Al. Who cares? It's a funny story. I love the visual of all of you dressed up like that."

"No, Tiffany, seriously. I know you think it's ridiculous, and it is. But just don't say anything more, please."

"I'm not swearing *my*self to secrecy. But don't worry; I won't say you told me. Have a Bloody Mary, Al, you'll feel better."

Al did not feel better.

That night the four of them dined on the terrace overlooking the Atlantic. Listening to the waves crashing on the sand and being lulled by generous amounts of superb wine, Daphne was beginning to open her mind to the Varley's. What made her think so harshly of them? She couldn't remember. They laughed appreciatively at Al's jokes and flattered her by writing down her recommendations for restaurants in Paris. Even though Chuck blew his nose in the napkin and Tiffany had the most irritating behavior toward her staff, alternating between being too chummy and too frosty, Daphne was finding them, if not delightful, at least bearable, even saying to Al while enjoying a last glass of Champagne before going to bed that night, "I am so sorry I avoided the Varley's all these months. I see why you like them so much. This was a perfect evening."

Fuzzy as her thinking was at that moment, Daphne recognized her own hypocrisy and remembered Arabella quoting Socrates. 'The unexamined life is not worth living.' Maybe she would examine her life one day, but not tonight.

The weather on Saturday was unusually hot, and Daphne left the pool-house right after breakfast to read in her room. Dozing off, she was awakened by Chuck's raised voice coming from the library.

She could not make out the words, but the message was delivered in staccato, commanding tones. "I would hate to be on the other end of that line," she thought vaguely as she looked around for her watch and decided it was time to get dressed and join Tiffany and Al at the pool for lunch.

Her blue bikini fit her perfectly, but she felt shy in front of the Varley's and was glad she'd brought the Manuel Canovas cover-up. She pulled her bedroom door open just in time to see Chuck kick Tiffany's Yorkshire terrier viciously in the side. The poor creature yelped pitifully and skittered down the marble hall. Daphne stood framed in the doorway holding the dolphin-shaped doorknob. She could take one step forward and be in the hall to confront Chuck and defend the dog, or she could just stand there and hope Chuck would not see her. She held her breath, undecided. Chuck stepped back into the library and closed the door.

Storming to the pool, the long printed voile robe spiraling behind her, Daphne was propelled by the sheer force of her anger. Al and Tiffany looked up anxiously, feeling her energy. "Al, something's come up, and I have to get back to the city right away. Tiffany, I'm sorry to leave unexpectedly and sorry to leave you with two less guests for your party tonight, but something came up suddenly." Daphne did not miss the naked fury on Tiffany's finely sculpted features.

"Surely, someone else can take care of whatever it is for you, Daphne. We can send a car for your boys if that's what you'd like." Tiffany's honeyed tone was a tribute to her astounding self-control.

"No, I'm sorry. I have to go. It's nothing to do with the boys." *It's true*, Daphne thought. *People do resemble their dogs.* She could see the terrier in Tiffany and was willing to bet she looked quite a bit like Chugger, her boxer, just now.

"Do as you please." Tiffany's voice was toneless.

Once they were on the Long Island Expressway, Al managed to get Daphne to tell him what happened. He swallowed his disappointment. He'd just been telling Tiffany what a big hit she and Chuck had made with Daphne. He was predicting many more amicable weekends leading to Tiffany's social advancement in Daphne's hard to breech circle. Al resigned himself to spending the rest of the weekend in the city when Daphne said, "Why don't you go back for the party tonight and stay as planned? I have to start packing for Maine. Just drop me off and keep the car."

Al felt like he'd won the lottery. "If you're sure you don't want me, I'll call Tiffany from your house and tell her I'm coming." Al sighed, anticipating the rich taste of chilled Corton-Charlemagne glazing his throat with magic.

Chapter 11

Richard traveled to Chicago for the Fourth of July weekend, and Maggie was forty-one days clean and sober, looking and feeling great. It was exhilarating for Maggie to think that Richard Blake would be packing his suitcase, going to LaGuardia and flying to Chicago, just to see her.

Waiting at the gate for Richard, Maggie reluctantly admitted to herself she hoped for more than friendship. What she didn't anticipate was missing the moment of his arrival. She failed to see Richard coming toward her. Richard, thinking his own thoughts and not expecting her at the airport, walked right by with his carry-on slung over his shoulder. He went straight to the taxi stand and on to the Drake Hotel. After unpacking, he called Maggie at the office. He was told she had already left for the weekend.

Flustered when she realized the last passenger had left the aircraft, Maggie searched baggage claim and waited until there was no longer even one suitcase unclaimed from the New York flight. She assumed Richard had decided not to come and was on the verge of tears. Damn, she wanted Richard. She called the Drake from a pay phone expecting the worst, spirits soaring when the operator put her call through to his room. "Richard, you're here! I'm so glad." It took her a moment to re-adjust her thinking, "I'm just going to finish some errands, and I'll call you when I get home. I made a reservation for dinner at eight. Why don't you come to my apartment around seven-thirty, and we'll walk to the restaurant."

"Sounds good to me."

Thank God he's here, Maggie thought to herself. *And he doesn't ever have to know I was waiting at the airport like a lovesick cow. What's the matter with me? People can't fall in love over the phone. Or maybe they can but shouldn't.*

Maggie gave her address to the cab driver and fretted all the way home. It was the first time she'd missed having a driver's license. Her feelings for Richard were so unclear, so confused. All she wanted now was that feeling she had when she was behind the wheel of a car, that feeling of being in charge, accelerating and braking in rhythm with the traffic.

Maggie was flustered when the doorbell rang but Richard's teasing way smoothed her nerves, and they talked non-stop during the short walk to Spiaggia, which was crowded with well-dressed, animated people. After a short wait, they were shown to a table and sat side by side on the banquette. Maggie ordered Perrier with lemon. Richard, the same. Maggie smiled and said, "You know, Richard, your drinking won't get me drunk."

"Actually, I don't want a drink, thanks, Maggie. I went to my nephew's wedding in Greenwich last weekend. It may have cured me of ever drinking again."

"Tied one on?"

"Not me."

"Come on, Richard. You were totally wasted on Daphne's birthday."

"An anomaly - seven or eight months ago."

"So what happened at the wedding last weekend?"

"I ran into horrendous traffic and was too late to get to the church. So I went straight to the reception – it was at the club in a tent overlooking Long Island Sound. A perfect day with lots of sailboats. Everything was great until you got a look at some of the guests."

"Oh, weddings are always full of too much of everything."

"I guess. But since I had to drive back to the city, I didn't want to drink much. It wasn't so much the kids as their mothers who got to me."

"What do you mean?"

"All these attractive, well-dressed women in their late forties, early fifties slowly throwing away their allure. The mother of the bride started belly dancing. She must have planned it. She had a set of those little finger cymbals. She did this alone on the stage. Even though she's in great shape for her age, it was not a pretty sight, believe me. One of her kids came and talked her down."

"Mother of the bride?"

"Yeah. I hope it doesn't run in the family."

"Belly dancing or drinking?"

"Both. I don't know why it bothered me so much. My nephew is a good kid, but I think his wife's a disaster. But let's change the subject. I'm only really interested in Maggie Miller," he said smiling and putting his hand on hers.

Maggie responded to the seismic shift and twisted in her seat hoping to hide her silly grin. "Well," she said, "I have no exotic dancing skills myself, so you don't have to worry about any public performances of that nature, but you may have to worry about getting a waiter. I'm starving."

After dinner, they walked back to Maggie's apartment building hand in hand. The new moon rising in the violet sky was breathtaking, and the evening ended with a long embrace. Richard held her to him until all the fear drained out of her body. For the first time in a long time Maggie felt safe.

Daphne called Maggie early the next week. "How was your weekend? Mine was strange. And I miss the boys. They're already in Maine. At sleep-away camp 'til the rental starts."

"What was strange about your weekend?"

"We went to Al's friends, the Varley's, in Southampton

"Tell me about the Varley's."

"Totally sumptuous."

"But what're *they* like?"

"Like all financial celebrities."

"Well, are they nice?"

"Not really."

"Would you go back?"

"I'd rather have a spinal tap, actually."

"And the house? I haven't been out there since it was finished, but it looked amazing going up."

"Amazing is the right word. What about you?" Daphne didn't want to talk about her weekend.

"I had a good time, but the heat's horrible. Is your phone number in Maine the same as last year?" Maggie didn't want to talk about her weekend, either.

"Yes. I arrive on the 15th. And should be in great shape by the time you get there. I'm bringing a mountain bike and plan on biking for hours every day."

"Is Al going to be biking with you?"

"Not when you come."

"Just checking."

"Don't worry, Maggie. I'm beginning to see similarities between Al and Kenny, beyond the blond hair. I'm not going to make that same mistake twice."

"I'll call you before you leave." Maggie ended the call before saying anything about her real news and ended up calling Daphne right back.

"Daphne, look, I don't know how to tell you this, but I think I'm falling for your friend Richard."

"Richard Blake?" Daphne bristled.

"I know. I know. Incredible. He came here this weekend, and it just sort of happened."

"You didn't even tell me he was coming. How did this happen so fast?"

"It wasn't so fast, really. He's been calling me ever since your birthday. Eight months now. Then I saw him that night in January."

"But why didn't you tell me he was calling you?" *Is this ownership I'm feeling for Richard?*

"I'm sorry. I didn't mean to be hiding anything. It's just that at first there was nothing to say and when we had dinner in January and nothing happened, I didn't think anything ever would. I didn't even admit to myself that the phone calls were turning into something. It seemed so stupid to say to you, 'I'm talking to Richard on the phone.' Anyway, it's something now."

"I don't want you to get hurt, Maggie. Richard is a weird one when it comes to romance. Secretive."

"I know. But I'm crazy about him. I've never felt like this before. And don't tell me that's what I always say."

"I guess it's what we all say because it's true. Every time it's new and different. Richard's a great guy. You know I love him. He's my best male friend. It's just you're the first normal person he's ever been interested in."

"We talked about his love life."

"You did?"

"It's not as bad as you might think."

"Well, that's good to hear. I just want you both to be happy." And she did want that, didn't she?

"I want you to be happy, too, Daphne. And while I'm into true confessions, I want to tell you I've been going to AA everyday for the past six weeks. I haven't had a drink, and I've been meeting with that woman I told you about, Della. She's my sponsor."

"Well, I'm going to open a bottle of Champagne and dedicate it to you and Richard and Della." Daphne felt strangely bitter and abandoned. *What's the matter with me?* She wondered. *Everything's the matter with me.* She thought.

The mangos were ripe and plentiful in the farmer's market that Saturday in mid-July, and after the ten a.m. AA meeting, Maggie went with Della to her apartment to spend the day making chutney.

"I'm glad I came clean with Daphne about AA and Richard." Maggie was standing at the stove, busy sterilizing the jars in a stockpot of boiling water.

"It was the right time. You've made a commitment now. To both."

"Look, Della, I want to thank you for helping me do this A. A. thing."

"AA *is* do-able, Maggie. Millions of people succeed in this, and willingness is all that's required." Della was peeling the mangos, hands dripping with juice.

"Sometimes I still want a drink."

"Just because you want a drink doesn't mean you *have* to have one. You can think the drink through. You've had enough experience with drinking to know where it can and does lead you."

"It's just that I'm not that long on self-discipline."

"Discipline's just remembering what you want, Maggie."

"I do *not* want to go back to getting drunk, but I *would* like to drink socially."

"I'm sorry, Maggie, but that's like saying you would like to have blue hair grow naturally out of your head. You're naturally predisposed to alcoholism just as you're naturally a brunette. And there're many worse things. Think about it."

"Yeah, I guess."

"Whether or not you want to, you will change the world. Everyone does. For better or worse. The sober Maggie has a much better chance of making the world a better place than the drunk Maggie, and I'm sorry to tell you there's no in between – no Maggie who can drink a little bit sometimes. I know you still want to think that, but it's delusional."

"Tell it like it is, Della."

"Don't tell me you want me to sugar-coat everything for you."

"Of course not. It's just that you are so definite about all this."

"Alcoholism is a dangerous disease, Maggie. The pathology is that it is incurable, progressive and fatal. Get it? It's dangerous for you to drink. Dangerous for you and dangerous for others."

"Last night I dreamt I was driving drunk. *So* relieved when I woke up."

"You have to take this disease as seriously as it took you. And don't think you're the one exception to the rule. That 'unique-me' thinking can be fatal."

"I know. And I don't want to cause any more harm."

"You don't have to. You have a choice now."

The sun streamed in Della's kitchen window as the two women worked side by side in companionable silence. Maggie remembered reading somewhere that Mother Theresa said, "One must master oneself before one can be of service to others." Della was a prime example of this.

Once all the jars were sterilized, Maggie dried her hands and tossed the dishcloth aside. "You know, Della, I'm beginning to see you make a lot of sense."

Chapter 12

"I can't believe it's already November. Time's flying." Maggie had just filled Daphne in on the past couple of days, including news of Richard.

"Oh, Maggie, how romantic to go to Paris for Thanksgiving. That Richard's a dark horse. I never thought he would fall in love, but he's got all the symptoms now. So exciting! Where're you going to stay?"

"No idea. His travel agent is working that out. Popular place, Paris. Most hotels are booked. What're you planning for the boys?"

"They're going with Kenny and his parents to Disney World. And I'm going to Thomasville."

"Are you sure that's a good idea?"

"I want to meet this Ella Smyth. You know, the one who claimed to be Dad's daughter. I've been wanting to meet her for over a year now."

"Have you told her that?"

"No. I just want to turn up. I have an open round trip ticket to Tallahassee, but no place to stay."

"Don't you have any family friends you could stay with?"

"Not really. Uncle Ludlow has some friends, the Hamilton's."

"Do you know them?"

"No. They moved there after Mom sold the Plantation. I'm not sure if the inn is still there, but if it is, that's where I'll stay. The ticket's bought and the car's rented, so it's a happening thing."

"The kids must be so excited about going to Disney World."

"Let's not talk about it. I should be the one taking them. All this got out of control. The Lang's told the boys without consulting me, and I'm plenty pissed, but there it is. They have the legal right to see the boys."

"You could always come with us to Paris."

"Maggie, you're now officially insane. I would never do that to you two. Anyway, I want to go to Thomasville. I just feel 'naughty' not telling Uncle Ludlow."

"You should tell him. He might want to go with you."

"He definitely doesn't want me to have any contact with Ella Smyth."

"Then, why are you? Hasn't he always given you good advice?"

"Yes," Daphne said wearily. "He's always given me good advice, and I'm going anyway because I'm willful and stubborn."

Maggie laughed. "Daphne, you're the best. I would offer to go with you, but as you know, I've accepted a much better offer."

"I'm so happy for you, Magpie."

"What about Al? I forgot to ask you about Al."

"He's going to the Varley's. They're having a big house party in Southampton. To tell you the truth, we aren't seeing as much of each other anymore. Nothing dramatic. Just beginning to dwindle off."

"Music to my ears."

On Wednesday morning Daphne left New York and after landing in Tallahassee went straight to the Avis counter. She remembered the road to Thomasville and soon crossed the Florida-Georgia border. She was not expecting the emotions these piney woods conjured up. She thought of her father the way he was, or rather the way she thought he was before the call from Ella Smyth. She longed for him to be exactly the man she remembered and nothing more. Her memory was becoming hazy, and she wondered how, after all these years, she could suddenly feel estranged from her dead father whose memory had always been strong and clear.

It occurred to her she could just turn around and go back to the airport. This possibility spurred her to drive on. The phone company had provided the address she needed, and she drove directly to a white clapboard house with a deep front porch shaded by oaks and bordered by a bedraggled boxwood hedge. It was a rural area, but the number on the mailbox assured her she had reached her destination. It was only noon, yet she was worlds away from Manhattan.

The sound of the rental car's door closing shattered the silence. Her footsteps crunched on the gravel path. The smell of the boxwood struck her and carried her back twenty-one years to the day of her father's death. She was spending New Year's week with her parents on Beech Grove Plantation in Thomasville. Daphne had been practicing the Twist, when her mother came into her room and turned off the record player. She took Daphne's hand and led her to the flagstone terrace, which overlooked the sunken rose garden. Boxwood hedges outlined the rose beds; the bushes were covered with burlap protecting them from the January winds. It had just rained, and the scent of boxwood saturated the air.

Her mother put her arm around Daphne's shoulders. "Darling Daphne, I have some terrible news, and we must be brave. Your Daddy was killed in a shooting accident this morning. You and I are going to go back to New York together this afternoon to make arrangements for his funeral. We'll be strong for each other. I love you so much, and though we'll never forget Daddy, we must live on in the way he would want us to."

Daphne stood there next to her mother looking down on the frozen rosebushes. She was too stunned to cry, but she remembered wondering why she wasn't crying. Where were her tears? Surely she should be crying now. How could she be thinking of tears instead of shedding them? She remembered this running through her head. Then, she'd turned to her mother and held on, pressing her face into her mother's shoulder. A few moments later her tears came in torrents.

Pausing on the path leading up to Ella Smyth's house, Daphne came back to the present moment and inhaled the boxwood. She felt a rush of compassion for the twelve-year-old she had been.

Three steps up to the porch. Despite the coolness of the day, the front door stood open. Only a buckled and torn screen stood between her and the dark interior. She looked around. The garage doors were shut, and there were no cars in sight. Nearby, a dove was calling its mate. She rang the bell and heard footsteps before seeing the silhouette of a man coming toward her, pulling on a shirt.

"What do you want?" The man standing behind the screen door had a strong New York accent, spiked with hostility. Light brown hair curled up the nape of his neck.

"Hello, I'm here to see Ella Smyth."

"And who are you?"

"Sorry. I'm Daphne Hone."

"No Hones welcome here. Clear off this property."

"But, I've come from…"

"Something wrong with your hearing, lady? I said clear off. You're trespassing on private property. Move on."

"Please, you don't understand..."

She heard the shotgun click into place. He stepped out onto the porch, shotgun held diagonally across his body. He was barefoot, wearing jeans. The open shirt showed a tan, taut chest.

"Who's that, Jimmy?" A woman's honeyed drawl came from the back of the house.

"Nobody to bother you, Ella. Go back to sleep." He looked at Daphne through squinting eyes. "What is it you don't understand?" He motioned with the gun toward the car. "Move."

Shaken, Daphne drove toward town and pulled over to the side of the road before reaching a populated area. She felt lightheaded and leaned on the steering wheel, weighing her options. Since she was here, she thought she would drive up the driveway of Beech Grove Plantation to see her old house and then go to the airport where she'd take the next available flight to Atlanta, which would connect her to New York.

Looking around and getting her bearings, she figured it was less than a ten-minute drive to Beech Grove and wondered if the house would look the same. On the way to the plantation, she noticed that most of the land was posted; trespassers were warned to keep off. Not wanting further trouble, Daphne made a u-turn on the narrow dirt road and headed for the airport. No more trespassing today.

Once checked in, she headed for the small airport's only restaurant, sat at the bar and ordered an Irish coffee and a tuna sandwich. She had a three-hour wait. Just as the coffee arrived, a muscular man, dressed in a business suit, came in and sat one stool over from her. He nodded to the bartender, reached over and shook his hand.

"I missed the two-thirty to Atlanta, Ray, so you've got me for three hours. How 'bout I start with a Coke and see how it goes."

"You've got it, Lex."

Lex turned to Daphne, "It's always a pleasure to see a beautiful stranger in this dreary place. Usually, it's just me and Ray hanging around here at this time of day." He put out his hand. "Alexis Martin, private investigator, at your service."

"Hi, I'm Helen Jones," Daphne smiled as she lied. "I overheard you and it seems we're on the same plane to Atlanta." Daphne took a sip of her coffee, appreciating the warmth and congratulating herself on the quick thinking. Since, even after all these years, the name Hone was still recognized in these parts, it seemed wiser to spend the afternoon as a Miss Jones. "What an interesting profession. Are you going to Atlanta on a case?"

"No, actually, I'm going to New York for personal reasons. My twenty-two-year-old daughter has a small part in *Sweet Charity*, and I know these revivals don't last long on Broadway so I want to get there before it's too late."

"You must be so proud!"

"Well, I am, but I hope she'll settle down and get a real job."

"But acting is a real job."

"It's fine, if you have a trust fund."

Daphne felt herself blush. "It's a wonderful show. I saw it this summer. What part does she play?"

"She's just one of the nameless dancers."

"But to be on Broadway you have to be the best." Daphne shifted on the stool and faced Lex more directly.

"She's my one and only, and I certainly think she's the best. What do you think, Ray?"

"Definitely, the best. Courtney is a true Georgia peach." The bartender smiled at them.

"You're not from Tallahassee?" Daphne asked.

"Before Lex, here, formed his own outfit, he worked for the Georgia Bureau of Investigation in Thomas County. He's one of the best detectives in the State of Georgia or anywhere for that matter." Ray loved to brag about his friends.

Although Lex and Daphne read for most of the two flights, by the time the plane landed at LaGuardia, they had become somewhat acquainted. Lex wrote the phone number of his hotel on his business card and gave it to Daphne as they were deplaning.

Walking toward baggage claim, Lex said, "Give me your number, and I'll let you know if my daughter Courtney can get a ticket for you. I'll be here for three days, and I know Courtney will be busy. Maybe I could even buy you lunch, Helen."

Daphne didn't answer. She'd forgotten she was Helen to this man. Lex looked at her and said, "No need to explain."

"I want to, though. And I think you can help me. Professionally, I mean."

While waiting for their suitcases to come off the carrousel, Daphne worked up a tale. In the shared taxi, she said she was distantly related to a family named Hone and knew they had a connection to Thomasville. She could tell this man Lex seemed to recognize the name and wondered what else he knew. He was of an age that he could have been working in Thomas County when her father died. He listened to her carefully while she continued the story about wanting to find out more about them. Maybe her story sounded hollow, but it was late, and she'd had a long day.

She ended her explanation by saying, "I was in Tallahassee on business, and I almost went to Thomasville to check if they're still there."

Daphne was glad that the night covered her red face. She was not a good liar.

As the taxi sped toward Manhattan, Daphne looked to her left as they were crossing the Triborough Bridge. It was her favorite view of New York. "Oz," she whispered as the lights flashed by. It was nearly eleven when the cab drew up to Daphne's house.

"Why don't you make a list of specific questions you want answered, and give me a call next week at my office. Maybe I can help you." Lex did not mention getting together for lunch again. She thought he looked relived saying goodnight to her.

What specific questions *did* she have? What she really wanted to know was if her mother knew about the affair. That was probably not something a man like Lex Martin could find out. What was she really after here? She let herself into the empty house. Even the pets, Chugger and Jazz were away in a kennel. *Thank God, I am home.* The strain of the day had taken its toll. She went directly into the shower and let the warm water work its magic. The image of that man with his shotgun looped in her mind as she shampooed her long hair.

Daphne slept until nearly eleven on Thanksgiving morning. She lay in her bed and thought of possibilities for the day. Going out to Long Island to have lunch with Ludlow was out as she had already lied to him concerning her whereabouts, having told all interested parties that she was spending Thanksgiving in Palm Beach visiting friends. She reached out for her address book and idly flipped through the sections. Everyone would be busy or out-of-town. She admitted to herself she was glad Al was safely in Southampton with the Varley's. How could she have ever thought they would be the kind of people she would like?

The *New York Magazine* was on her bedside table. She picked it up and looked at the movies. She wanted to see *A Room with a View*, *The Color of Money* and *Crocodile Dundee*. Plenty of time to see all three. Nothing wrong with spending Thanksgiving at the movies. After telling so many lies she needed to sit in the dark and escape for the day.

The phone rang. It was Louisa calling from London.

"Happy Thanksgiving, Aunt Daphne. I'm calling to tell you I'm cooking my first turkey dinner. Fortunately, almost all my guests are English and won't know if I've screwed up or not."

"Almost all your guests? I hope that means you have a Rhodes scholar coming."

"It does. In fact, he's here helping me cook."

"I'm so happy, Louisa."

"Me, too. Got to go just wanted to say hello. Love you, Aunt Daphne."

Perched at her desk on Friday morning, Daphne called Lionel and asked him to pick up Chugger and Jazz from the kennel on his way in. She told him that the weather was lousy in Palm Beach and that she was so happy to be home.

"You should have called me to pick you up, Mrs. Hone."

"I got in late last night. Too late."

"Sorry you didn't have any sunshine. Hope you had a good Thanksgiving dinner, though."

"I did, Lionel, thanks. And I know you did. Your mother's such a good cook."

"We had a real Jamaican feast as you know we always do."

Daphne did not want anyone to know she had spent Thanksgiving eating popcorn. That would be her little secret with herself. Perceiving the trip to Thomasville as a failure, she preferred not thinking about it, but her mind kept coming back to the private detective. Lex Martin said to make a list of specific questions. Well, she would do just that. What were they, though? She opened the long middle drawer of her desk and got out a notebook and a felt tipped pen. "Who was shooting at Beech Grove Plantation on the day of the accident? What were the results of the inquest? Any extenuating circumstances?"

Thinking back, Daphne remembered New Year's of 1966 when they had all been in Thomasville. She had always thought her father was out shooting with some friends as he often did. That would not have been an unusual occurrence, but was it fact or assumption? She didn't know. As it turned out, she and her mother left the plantation that afternoon and never went back. Until now those memories were pristinely frozen in time, but now they were melting into a chaotic blur, destabilizing her world. Daphne squirmed in the desk chair.

Looking at her short list, she thought how odd it was she didn't know the answers to these simple questions. All these years had gone by, and only now did she see the uncertainty. She thought of calling Johnny and asking him what he remembered. He had been thirty-two at the time and would surely know all the facts. It was three in the afternoon in London, a good time to call, but she didn't reach for the phone. She had a funny feeling he didn't know the truth, either.

Instead, she wrote a letter to Lex Martin with her questions and asked him to take her case. She said she would call him at the end of the following week for his answer and intentionally did not include her phone number. Signing the letter Helen Jones, she thought how irritating it would be to keep up this ruse. She would have to pay him by money order and make sure he did not call her. She did not want to take the chance that the phone would be answered "Hone Residence." She was not sure why, but she did not want him to know she was the daughter of John Hone. She also did not want Uncle Ludlow or Maggie to know about Lex Martin, but she mailed the letter anyway. What a tangled, tangled web she was weaving.

Later that afternoon, Maggie called from Paris. "Daphne, you're home. I have joyous news!"

"Let's hear it."

"Richard and I are getting married!"

"Hooray! I'm so happy for you both. You've changed my dreary day to sunshine."

"Aren't you were supposed to be in Thomasville this weekend? What happened?"

"Oh, nothing. Just a change of plan. I didn't even see Ella Smyth. I don't know what I was thinking of going down there like that. But I'm not going to think about that anymore. From now on, I'm only going to think about what I am going to wear to your wedding."

"Oh, Daphne, I'm so excited," Maggie continued. "We just told my parents. They're thrilled. They think the world of Richard. We're going to get married soon but without a lot of fanfare."

"Don't even *think* you're getting married without my being the matron of honor and both boys bearing the ring or rings!"

Maggie laughed, and Richard got on the phone. "As you now know, I'm the luckiest man in the world. But I don't have time to talk. I'm trying to find out if Maggie is in favor of diamond rings. See you next week."

Daphne sat at her desk and let the delight in their voices sink down into her heart. This was indeed wonderful news. Of course she was happy for her friends, but at the same time, she felt left out. It frustrated her to admit to this childish reaction, and her eyes stung. She reached for the phone. She would call the boys at their hotel in Orlando and tell them about the upcoming marriage with joy in her voice.

Chapter 13

A week later a letter arrived from Alexis Martin addressed to Helen Jones. Of course he was just playing along with the Helen Jones thing. He must know she was lying. Why did she think for a moment she could fool a detective? She slit the letter open with a slender silver paper knife. She blushed as she read, "Dear Helen". He wrote that he was too busy to help her at this time. He wished her well and said that he had enjoyed meeting her. That was it. Daphne wasn't used to being brushed off and consoled herself by thinking that she was not herself that day after being threatened with a shotgun. She could always get another detective. She looked over at the Yellow Pages sitting on a shelf.

Now that she had made a list of specific questions, they haunted her, staying at the surface of her consciousness. Who did she know with the name of a good private investigator? A discreet person who would ask no questions? The answer was, of course, Ludlow.

She picked up the phone. "Uncle Ludlow, I have a friend who needs a private detective. Can you give me the name of someone reliable?"

"I know a few. Do you know if this case requires international travel and languages?"

"I don't really know, but I would think not."

"Well, if it does Tom Flagg's your man. In fact, he's your man anyway. I'll stop by your place on my way home and say hello to you and the boys. I'll get his number and bring it with me."

That was easy, she thought, and she didn't have to call this Tom Flagg. She could wait and see. But wait and see what? She was consumed with curiosity and felt it was her duty to know these things.

Why had she accepted so little information for all these years? Guessing she could call the Sheriff's office in Thomasville, but not feeling comfortable doing that, she read the letter from Lex Martin again. She should have dropped him off at his hotel if she had wanted to be anonymous. Too late. But even so, why didn't he take the case? She hadn't said there was any urgency. He could have agreed to take it when his caseload was lighter.

The following morning, she called Flagg's office at nine a.m. He answered the phone on the first ring.

"Mr. Flagg, this is Daphne Hone. Ludlow Fowler recommended you to me."

"If you are a friend of his then that recommends you to me, as well."

"Actually, in this case, I would appreciate it if he didn't know I'm the client. I told him a friend needed your services."

"Of course. I never discuss my cases, Mrs. Hone." Daphne liked the sound of his voice.

"Let me explain. My father was killed in a shooting accident in Thomasville, Georgia, on January 4th 1966. I was twelve at the time and was never told anything more than that he was killed in an accident. I would like to know everything you can find out about that day. He was a close friend of Ludlow's and I think Ludlow may be 'protecting' me from some information." No more subterfuge, Daphne thought.

"Why don't you come to my office where we can discuss this further? I'm free at two this afternoon. Is that convenient for you?"

"I'll be there, Mr. Flagg."

Daphne felt uncomfortable with Tom Flagg. For one thing, he was too handsome, but she liked his direct manner and was glad he could take the case right away. She told him about Ella Smyth and the young man with the shotgun. He told her he would go to Thomasville later that week and could possibly have a preliminary report in two or three week's time.

"I'm an adult now, Mr. Flagg, and I want to know all the circumstances of the accident and whatever you can find out about my father's personal life as well." They signed the contract and made an appointment for the follow-up. Daphne left his office feeling buoyant that she had taken this step. Something nagged her, though. Maggie had pointed out that Ludlow had always given her good advice in life, and here she was deceiving him through secrecy.

Daphne stepped out into the December afternoon and headed for the Mayfair Hotel where she was meeting Maggie for tea at four.

"And what have you been up to this sunny afternoon, Daphne?" Maggie looked radiant with an irrepressible smile.

"I have done absolutely nothing but think about your wedding. I'm so glad you're taking me up on having it at my house, and even though I think Valentine's day is corny, if that's what you want, then I'm all for it. How do you tell people you are getting married on February 14th with a straight face?"

"I don't tell them with a straight face. I laugh, and they laugh, and I'm so, so happy!"

Daphne smiled at her friend. "The wedding is my present to you two."

"Oh, Daphne, thank you so much. My mother will make a fuss that she should be doing it, but really she'll be relieved, and so am I."

"Now the real question is would you like to choose the food and flowers or would you rather be surprised?"

"I would rather be surprised. I can't think of anything except Richard and how happy I am. And, of course, I have to talk to my probation officer and get out of the Chicago apartment and look for an apartment here and wonder how I'm going to tell the bank that it's over between us. So you see I have no time for wedding plans and am so lucky to have you as my best friend!"

"What do you mean about telling the bank it's over?"

"I'm going to the Gemological Institute of America in April to take the same gem identification course you took and maybe a diamond grading one, too. Then maybe I'll understand Richard's business well enough to make myself useful. I'm so sick of banking. It was the wrong choice for me."

"You'll love the jewelry business and be good at it, too. Did you find a dress today?"

"Yes. At Bergdorf's. And it's very bride-y. Ruffles and all. Not really me, but I love it."

"When can I see it?"

"I have a fitting on Monday at eleven. Come with me, and we can have lunch somewhere fancy afterwards. To celebrate. And what are you going to wear to the wedding?"

"I found a Zandra Rhodes dress at Martha. Looks like something out of 'A Mid-summer's Night Dream'. I'll look amazing, so look out!"

"Oh, you won't out-do me! I'll have a long tulle veil sprinkled with silk lilies-of-the-valley. And shoes embroidered with same."

"I think you'll be the best bride ever."

"I expect so."

That evening after dinner with her sons, Daphne went to her room with a glass of wine. She hated having secrets from Maggie and Ludlow. It was early so she called Arabella Yamada.

"Arabella! Haven't seen you in too long. Any chance we can have lunch tomorrow? I need your advice."

"I would love to have lunch with you, dear. Why don't you come here, and we'll order room service."

"Great. I'll be there at noon."

Daphne cruised down to the kitchen several times that night to refill her wine glass.

Walking up Fifth Avenue to the Sherry Netherland Hotel from her office, Daphne shivered in her tweed coat. The weather had turned and the cold wind had stripped the leaves from the trees. It had rained earlier and the leaves lay dead and sodden in the gutters.

Riding up to the thirty-seventh floor with the white-gloved elevator operator, Daphne commented, "What a wind whipping across the Park today! I think it's colder on this corner than anywhere else in the City."

"That's what they say, Miss. I just think it has the cleanest air."

Arabella's apartment was small and perfect, and Daphne was glad to feel her warmth and welcome. The bright Chinese yellow living room had two windows over-looking the Park and the Plaza Hotel, and a third looked down Fifth Avenue directly at the huge holiday snowflake in front of Tiffany's. The phone rang as Arabella was taking Daphne's coat, and Daphne stood at the window while Arabella took the call in her bedroom.

Daphne looked down at Central Park and thought how bleak the trees looked, just black blobs from this height. It was a distant view, and still she felt a sadness. She remembered loving tree skeletons in years past, like sculptures, she'd thought, but today she didn't like the way they made her feel and couldn't shake her mood. She had a longing for something, but she couldn't put her finger on what it was. A sort of vague and dismal discontent weighed heavily around her heart. She turned her back on the window just as Arabella stepped back into the room.

"Sorry, Darling. That was Maggie telling me about the wedding. I'm so pleased she invited me. So nice of you to have it at your house. And such fun to have it on Valentine's."

"It's not at all like Maggie or Richard to be romantic, like that. I can't believe they chose Valentine's except it will help Richard remember their anniversary. It makes my job as event planner easy, though. It's going to be all hearts – totally corny, but fun."

"I'm going to wear red to be in the spirit of it. I've already ordered lunch for us. It should arrive in a few minutes. Tell me what's on your mind."

"You're the only person I can talk to, Arabella. I have gotten myself into an awkward situation, and I've been keeping secrets from Uncle Ludlow and Maggie. It's really bothering me."

"What's it about?"

"About my father. I went down to Thomasville and came back with some questions so I've hired a private detective to do some research on his death and his personal life. Please keep this between us."

Did Arabella blanche or did Daphne imagine it?

"That's ancient history, Daphne, why would you want to do that?"

"I think it's my right, and even my duty, to know as much as I can."

"Daphne, maybe your father, even though he's dead, has a right to his privacy. I don't know, but I can tell you, I would not like anyone snooping around in my life after I'm dead."

"Are you telling me I shouldn't be doing this?"

"Well. I'm just saying that it's often best to let sleeping dogs lie."

"Ever since Ella Smyth called Johnny, I've been wondering about what happened back then, and I want to know the truth."

"Why don't you ask Ludlow? He would know."

"I think he is hiding something from me."

"Daphne, dear, all this happened so long ago. Let the past stay in the past. You have two wonderful sons. Just enjoy them and don't go digging around."

"I was hoping for your support."

The doorbell rang. The waiter came in with a silver-domed cart and silently set up a table in a corner of the room. "Luncheon is served, Madame Yamada."

"Thank you, Pierre. Daphne, I hope you like Peking Duck. It's been my favorite since childhood."

"Oh, you San Franciscans are so sophisticated. When I was a kid, we only liked creamed chicken in New York."

The two women talked of other things, and Daphne felt disappointed. Just as she was about to leave, Arabella remarked, "Your private investigator. His name isn't, by any chance, Tommy Flagg, is it?"

Dumbfounded, Daphne just nodded.

"His mother was a very glamorous character."

"Tell me about her."

"She was much younger than I am. About your mother's age. Mary Flagg, from Philadelphia, originally. I knew her fairly well. We were in the same book club here in New York. She was a beautiful, vivacious woman."

"What happened?"

"Cancer. I went to her funeral and was very impressed with her son. Ludlow was there, and he dropped me home."

"Please don't say anything about this to Uncle Ludlow."

"I won't Daphne, but I hope you know what you are doing."

Daphne was fascinated that Arabella knew Tom Flagg's mother, but it did not dispel her gloom. She went to F. A. O. Schwartz and bought too many Christmas presents trying to cheer herself up, then dragged herself home still feeling melancholy. There was a message from Tom Flagg saying that something had come up and that he could not meet with her until mid-January. He did not say if what had come up pertained to her case or not. She called his office number and got a recorded message saying he was unavailable until after the New Year, except in an emergency. The emergency number had a 201 area code. Daphne heaved a sigh and promised herself to forget about this and concentrate all her energy on making Christmas merry.

Chapter 14

By the middle of January 1987, Chuck Varley had become the talk of New York. He was under investigation by the SEC and people started discussing money constantly. Who was making it. Who was losing it. Daphne had never noticed people talking about money so much before, but now they could talk of nothing else. Daphne listened and waited for a phone call from Tom Flagg.

It came early one morning as she was just about to head out to her office. "Mrs. Hone? Tom Flagg here. I have a report for you, and I apologize for the delay."

"When can we meet?" She considered telling him about Arabella knowing his mother, but decided this was not the time.

"How about tomorrow morning around eight-thirty at my office?"

"Fine. See you then."

There was a manila envelope on Flagg's desk. "Mrs. Hone…"

"Please call me Daphne."

"Daphne, I remembered what you said about being an adult and wanting the truth of what happened twenty-one years ago. This report contains the facts as well as some hearsay. I included everything, but as you will see, the hearsay is clearly marked."

"Thank you, Tom."

"You can take this home or read it here in the so-called conference room. I don't think it will take more than an hour to read, and I'm available either way to answer any questions."

"I'm sure it's clear, and thank you for the offer of reading it here. I'd like that."

Flagg showed Daphne into the adjacent room. The walls were book lined. Dark green leather armchairs surrounded an oval mahogany table in the center. The room had an odd sort of coziness, and Daphne settled in to read.

My poor, sweet mother, she thought after reading the report. *It seems I never knew my father at all.* Daphne thought back to her childhood. Her mother had protected her from ever guessing the truth about her father. She had let Daphne keep him as her hero. Daphne's emotions roller-coasted. Did Johnny know the kind of man their father was? Why was Ludlow such a loyal friend? All this information, so many years later, was confusing. She sat still and let it sink in.

Nearly two hours had passed before she knocked on the door, which separated the two rooms, more of an announcement than expecting it to be opened. She went in and sat down facing the detective. "Well, Tom, this was a big surprise. I never even considered that my father's death might have been murder."

Tom Flagg looked at her nodding his head, waiting for her to continue.

"You think this guy, Jimmy, who pulled a shotgun on me, you think his father murdered my father. The jealous husband?"

"I don't have an opinion on this, Daphne. I found out that your father was having an affair with Jimmy's mother, Loretta Healy who was married at the time to Ed Healy, and that it was rumored that Jimmy was your father's child. Mr. Healy has a history of violence and didn't have an alibi on the morning of your father's death, although he was never formally accused. As you now know, it was ruled a suicide, but there were extenuating circumstances."

"I never even knew it was ruled a suicide. I always thought it was an accident. No one ever discussed it with me. Of course, I was just a child."

"You were only twelve-years-old, and you lived in New York, well away from all the publicity."

"My mother sold the place, and we never went back. She did what she thought was best. She always tried to protect me."

Again, Tom sat nodding waiting for Daphne.

"And this man, Alexis Martin, must have been very young at the time. He resigned from the Sherriff's office because of this case and moved on to the Georgia Bureau of Investigation, is that right?" Daphne asked.

"Right. Word got around that he believed it was murder and that Ed Healy had done it. He made some semi-public remarks which would have made it difficult for him to stay on as a Deputy."

"He talked about Ed Healy being the Sherriff's nephew?"

"He didn't have to. That was public knowledge. Lex Martin was young, as you pointed out, and let's just say he wanted justice to be done. He was passionate about justice."

"What happened to him?"

"Sadly, this case became a blot on his career. He's a fine detective, but he was too outspoken and even though he did good work for the GBI, the Sherriff of Thomas County made sure he didn't last long there. He's an independent now, like me."

"By a really strange coincidence, I met him at the Tallahassee airport." Daphne didn't want to say anything more about it. She'd put that pack of lies behind her and did not want to go into it with Tom Flagg.

"Mind if I use your phone, Tom?"

"Please, go right ahead. There's an extension in the conference room, if you want some privacy."

"No. This won't take long." Arabella answered her private line right away, "Hi. It's Daphne. May I come over for a few minutes?" Daphne replaced the receiver.

"Tom, I need some time to digest all of this. I may have more questions and will be in touch with you soon. Thank you for doing such a thorough job."

Tom Flagg walked Daphne to the elevator and waited with her until it came. Upset though she was, she noticed his impeccable manners and appreciated his tact.

It was only a ten-minute walk from Flagg's office to the Sherry Netherland. Daphne's mind was still reeling, and by the time Arabella opened the door, she was bursting with questions.

"I have just come from Tom Flagg's office, and you *won't believe* what I've found out. Why on earth did my mother stay with my father?"

"Let me take your coat and get you a sherry, dear. I think I can explain some things to you."

"Yes. I need some answers." Daphne tried to keep the anger out of her voice.

Arabella handed Daphne a small glass of pale amber liquid and took her coat.

"Your father was not always a philanderer," she began. "He and your mother had ten good years together before his drinking got bad and he started spending his evenings away from home. I had only just met your mother at the time of the accident..."

"Don't say accident. Call it what it was."

"Suicide."

"No. Murder."

"Murder? I never heard anything about murder." Arabella was stunned.

Daphne handed over the manila envelope. "If you don't mind, Arabella, I'm going to ask you to read this so we can discuss it. I need to sit here quietly and write down some questions while you read. May I have a pad and pencil?"

Daphne and Arabella sat in the Chinese yellow living room in silence. It was nearly noon by the time Arabella finished reading the forty-page report.

She looked up and said, "I didn't know any of this. I always thought it was suicide. Your mother did confide in me about her marriage, though, so I can answer some of your questions, at least. But not all. So sorry, dear, all this must come as a terrible shock to you."

"It *is* shocking, but I don't want to exaggerate it. I want to keep in perspective that this happened over twenty years ago." Daphne got up and helped herself to another glass of sherry from a brass table in the corner, which held an array of decanters, bottles and glasses.

"I don't mean to add to today's surprises," Arabella continued, "but I actually met this Loretta Healy and her son, Jimmy. They came to your mother's house a couple of times while I was there, before she became ill. Your mother sent Loretta money from time to time. I know that Loretta Healy moved with her son to Brooklyn to be close to her parents after your father's death and her divorce from Ed Healy."

"I sort of met him when I went to Thomasville."

"He was a surly kid."

"Well, he's a surly adult, now," Daphne said.

"But Loretta was nice, and your mother said Jimmy looked a little like your father, but not enough to say for sure whose child he was. Apparently, Ed Healy looked somewhat like your father. Younger, though."

"I can't believe you know all this."

"I was there with your mother at the time. Even though we had just met, or I should say, probably *because* we had just met, she confided in me things she might not have said to others who knew the whole cast of characters. I think she was glad she could talk to someone who was not enmeshed with all these people."

Daphne picked up the folder. "So. This report says Loretta remarried, and since Jimmy doesn't get on with and often fights with his new stepfather, he went down to Georgia to find his real father, Ed Healy, who is now in the State hospital for the insane. It's this Jimmy, Loretta's son, who is now living with my Dad's ex-girlfriend's daughter, Ella Smyth. And the two of them came up with the plan to claim *she* was my father's daughter. Some family, I've got, right?"

"Daphne, all this looks terrible on paper. Tommy's report focuses on the dramatic incidents of the last few years of your father's life. It doesn't mention the good times, the trips to the Grand Canyon or Europe or Disneyland or any of the nice things he did with you. Even though your mother knew he was a binge drinker, she said that he could be fine for months at a time and then drink and go crazy for a few days or weeks."

"I just don't know what to do." Daphne poured a little more sherry into the small, stemmed glass.

"I suggest you do nothing. And if you ask me, I would say don't mention to Ludlow that you've had all these secrets unearthed. He has been keeping them for a long time, thinking that it was in your best interest. He's an old man. Don't upset him. And for that matter, why bring it up with Johnny, either? You're in possession of all the facts. What more do you want?"

"Are you mad at me for stirring this up?"

"I could tell the last time we talked you needed to find out what happened. I might've thought before I read this report that I could've filled you in on everything, but I can see that I only knew part of what happened."

"But what about justice?"

"Daphne, the suspect is in a mental hospital. Leave it alone."

"But I don't want people to think my father committed suicide if he didn't."

"People outside of Thomasville heard it was an accident, and those in Thomasville who still remember the case will remember the extenuating circumstances. Leave it alone, Daphne. Bringing this back will only cause harm for you and the boys."

"I don't see how bringing out the truth will harm us," said Daphne as she poured a little more sherry.

"You've had a shock today. Don't say anything to anyone for a week, and then come back. We'll talk about it then."

"You've got a deal, Arabella. May I invite myself for lunch a week from today."

"Of course, dear. I'll look forward to that."

Daphne felt a bit unsteady as Arabella helped her on with her coat, but her head cleared when she hit the bitter January air. She walked slowly toward her office in the weak winter sun trying to make sense of the past.

A week later Daphne rang Arabella's doorbell at noon.

How do you feel now?" Arabella looked at Daphne with kindness and compassion.

"You were right. I don't want to tell anyone about this. The other night, I had a little bit too much to drink, and I got telephonitis and tried to call both Maggie and Al, but thank God, neither of them were home."

"Maybe you should watch your drinking, dear. Alcoholism is genetic. Also incurable, progressive and fatal."

"Oh, I don't binge drink. Maggie's still going to AA, though. I miss her. She's always busy with Richard now, of course, but still."

"I understand. When a friend gets married, the dynamics of the relationship change for a little while, but she will always be your closest friend after all these years."

"I guess that's why Uncle Ludlow kept those secrets about Dad. They were college roommates. He wanted me to remember Dad in the best light."

"Of course. And you should, too. Your father had many fine qualities."

"I know. This week I have been remembering all the good times. In fact, I don't think I ever saw him drunk. And I've decided it's best never to tell his secrets. I'm always going to refer to his death as an accident. I don't know what I was thinking about last week. Thank you for your restraint and wisdom."

"I knew you would understand after you had a chance to get used to the information. And you're right, Ludlow wants to protect his friend, even in death. That's what a loyal friend does."

"Dad was lucky to have Ludlow. We are all lucky to have him. I wonder just how much of all this Johnny knows?"

"He was living in London by then, so my guess is he thinks it was suicide. He was an adult so I am sure he knew what the ruling was. I never heard a breath of murder until I read the report, and I only knew about the ruling because your mother told me. For many reasons, the word was that it was an accident. I always respected that and never told a soul."

"I suppose *I'm* those many reasons."

"Well, maybe most. People get nosey and want to know too many things and talk about suicide more than an accident. Don't forget this happened in 1966. There was a stigma attached to suicide then. "

"Much less now."

"Of course."

"But the whole thing's horrible. Jealous husband. Crime of passion." Daphne said. "I just hope it happened quickly, and Dad didn't see it coming."

"The positive action you can take now is to put this behind you and concentrate on having fun with your sons and do whatever it is that you have to do in preparation for Maggie's wedding. Please don't stay stuck in 1966."

"I'm ahead of the game as far as wedding plans go. Just the last minute things left. But you're right. I went and dug up the past and what I really need to do is carve out a future with good memories for Henry and Joe. I've been thinking I'd like to take them to Williamsburg, and I'm going to invite Uncle Ludlow to go with us. And you! What about you? Why don't we all go on President's weekend?"

"I'd love to go. Count me in. You know, Mary Flagg was on the Colonial Williamsburg Foundation board, and I think Tommy took her place when she died. Why don't you ask him how best to plan that trip?"

"Arabella, you're a fount of information. And I want to thank you so much for being my mother's loyal friend."

"I still miss her, you know."

"Me, too. Especially this week."

Later that afternoon, Daphne called Tom Flagg. "Tommy, I'm calling on a matter for the future rather than the past."

"Good news. And how do you know I'm called Tommy?"

"You're the detective."

"This may be out of my league. But I know people who can make you talk."

Daphne laughed, "Arabella Yamada was my mother's closest friend."

"She's a great lady. I don't know her well, but I'd like to. Now, what can I do for you?"

"Arabella told me you're a big deal in Williamsburg. Is there anyway you can help me? I'd like to take a family trip there on President's weekend."

"This year?"

"Yes. Is that possible?"

"Maybe. By chance, I'm going down there myself on President's weekend for some meetings. How many bedrooms do you want?"

"Four."

"That's a tall order. Let me see what I can do and get back to you."

Later that night, Maggie called Daphne. "What's going on?"

"I had lunch with Arabella today."

"I'm so glad she's coming to the wedding."

"And while you're honeymooning, we're all going to Williamsburg for President's weekend. That would be Uncle Ludlow, Arabella, the boys and me. Plus there's a mystery man you know nothing about."

"Come on, Daphne. I can't stand not knowing."

"Someone handsome. Who knows Arabella and Ludlow, slightly, but still. Who has an interesting career. Who's successful. Who's an actual grown-up. Totally radical for me."

"I'm going to throw you my bouquet."

"Definitely a good idea."

Chapter 15

At noon on Valentine's Day the clergyman from St. James' Church stood with Richard in front of a roaring fire in Daphne's living room waiting for the bride. The convivial sound of sixty chatting voices spattered out onto the street as the black limousine pulled up in front of Daphne's house with Maggie and her parents. All the furniture in the living room was pushed against the walls, and the guests were standing or sitting, as best they could.

The garden was tented in red canvas with thin white stripes ready for the luncheon after the ceremony. It was filled by eight red skirted round tables for six and one long table for twelve, the tables littered with heart-shaped candies and every sort of red flower held in what looked like lace. There was no space for a band, but the Italian accordionist was cheerful and seemed to know every tune.

Henry, almost ten now, and Joe, just turned seven, were standing at the open front door signaling to the accordionist that the bride had arrived. Mendelssohn's Wedding March started up, and all conversation stopped as Maggie floated up the curving stairs. Richard marveled at the utter perfection of Maggie, as her father guided her to his side.

While Daphne held Maggie's bouquet during the exchange of rings, her mind drifted back to earlier in the day. She wasn't sure how she felt about Al, who had purposefully made himself obvious by directing the catering staff and loudly welcoming the people he knew and introducing himself to others. She looked over at him. He was certainly handsome. Tall and blond, composed and perfectly tailored. He could, and often did, drive her crazy, and today his bossiness with the wait-staff annoyed her, but she was glad he had taken care of Della, who had flown in from Chicago.

Daphne's thoughts churned on. *This Della woman probably just came here to make sure Maggie doesn't have even a sip of Champagne on her wedding day. So weird of Maggie to invite an AA person to her wedding.*

Al had introduced Della around while Daphne busied herself with other guests. Della was gorgeous, Daphne had to give her that. And chic. *Who would have thought some ex- drunkard from Chicago could look so good?* Daphne's mind came back to the ceremony just in time to give Maggie back the bouquet and resume her role as hostess.

Quickly straightening Maggie's veil, Daphne darted down-stairs to check the tent. The heaters had been too efficient, and she opened one of the flaps to cool it down before the guests were seated for luncheon. Surveying the scene was calming. It couldn't have been prettier. Just like an old-fashioned Valentine card, she thought.

Still standing at the entrance to the tent, Daphne nodded and smiled at the waiter as she took a flute of Perrier-Jouët Rosé Champagne from the tray. It tasted delicious, cold and just dry enough. The guests were still upstairs, and she should herd them down, but not yet. She wanted to savor this rare Champagne and listen to the laughter from afar. Her two best friends now married to each other! She sincerely wanted to be happy about it.

She lingered there a little longer, half in the empty entrance hall, half in the tent. There was no room for her in the kitchen, and she was not ready to join the party upstairs. She finished her Champagne and vaguely looked around for a place to leave the glass. This is ridic-ulous, she thought, and scooped up the skirts of her fairytale dress and took the stairs two at a time.

She bumped right into Della at the top of the stairs. "Daphne, I'm Della, Maggie's friend from Chicago. Your house is beautiful, and I have never been to such a wonderful wedding! It's so cozy, yet elegant at the same time. I don't know how you did it."

"Hello, how are you?" Daphne managed. "Maggie quotes you all the time. I expected you to be much older with all that wisdom." Daphne thought the sarcasm was not audible in her voice.

"Oh that Maggie is the best! She's brought a lot of laughter to my life, and as you know, she's your devoted and loyal friend."

Daphne wondered what secrets might have been shared. Maggie was fully aware of where the skeletons were buried and who knew what she might have said to this woman.

"Della, forgive me. I see my uncle over there, and I have something important to tell him." Daphne made a beeline for Ludlow who was chatting with Arabella.

"Thank goodness you two are here. You've got to keep that woman away from me and help me push these party people down to the tent."

"Right. Great party, Daphne." Ludlow put his hand Daphne's shoulder.

Arabella, dressed in a red Valentino suit smiled at Daphne. "Everything's perfect, dear. Your mother would be proud. I love that it's all red and white and lacey. By the way, I'm looking forward to our 'family' weekend. I heard from Tommy, and he was able to get two double rooms at the Williamsburg Inn and two singles at some place nearby. Ludlow and he are taking the singles, and you and I will sort it out with the boys. It was the best he could do at such short notice."

"Oh, Arabella, it was *you* who got Tom involved. I was wondering how Tom figured in this event." Ludlow said. The women caught each other's eyes. Daphne willed Arabella to keep her secret.

"When Daphne mentioned wanting to go to Williamsburg, I remembered that Tommy had taken Mary's place on the board." Arabella said while looking around the room.

"Trust a woman to figure these things out. Daphne, you'll like Tom. Did your friend ever use his services?" Ludlow asked.

"No idea. Only passed on his name. I was surprised when Arabella brought him up in connection with Williamsburg, and I'm *really* looking forward to our trip. It'll be fun, and I'm glad it's soon. This wedding was a lot more work than I bargained for."

Arabella put her hand on Ludlow's arm and turned to Daphne, "Would you like us to go down to the tent and settle in and hope the others will follow?"

"Yes, please. So hard to get people moving." Daphne looked relieved.

When the time came to throw the bouquet, no one could find Daphne. It was Henry who went to her room and found her sitting on the loveseat in her bedroom, stroking the cat. Chugger was asleep in front of the fire. "Come on, Mom. Maggie's ready to throw her bouquet. Everyone's looking for you."

Daphne knew Henry had noticed the clear Champagne bottle with the pink flowers on it sitting on the floor next to her. It was nearly empty.

"I'm tired. And I don't want to catch the bouquet. Tell them to go on without me."

"Mom. Maggie's your best friend. It's her wedding. She told me to come find you. Her mother's drunk."

"What a thing to say, Henry. You don't even know what drunk is."

"I do too know. It's like you, right now."

Daphne could feel the blood leap to her face and the muscles in her arm tightened, ready to slap him hard, but she stopped herself.

"Get out of my sight right now and make sure that bouquet doesn't get anywhere near me." Henry ran out slamming the door behind him.

Energized by her anger, Daphne repaired her makeup, downed some Binaca and raced downstairs, ready to take charge.

Maggie threw her bouquet directly to Della who caught it with the most enchanting smile. Daphne was astonished. Helping herself to another glass of Champagne, she took Maggie aside, and in a quiet, nasty voice said, "After all I've done for this wedding, that bouquet was *mine*. Remember?"

"Oh, Daphne, I'm so sorry. Henry just now came to me and said you didn't want it."

"I can't believe you'd listen to *him*. He's in high 'I-hate-my-mother' mode."

"How can you say that? He adores you and is so concerned."

"Concerned? Concerned about what?" Caged rage was billowing out of every pore.

Knowing Daphne was drunk and that it would be impossible to reason with her, Maggie tried to calm her down. It was her wedding day, and she didn't want an argument. All she wanted now was to leave the reception and go to Nassau on her honeymoon with her husband.

"I'll be back in two weeks," she said soothingly. "You know you can call the Lyford Cay Club anytime day or night. If you want me, call me. On another note, no one has ever had a more perfect wedding. I'm filled with admiration and love for you, Daphne, and for everything you did for me today. Thank you for always being my best friend in the whole wide world."

Maggie hugged Daphne for longer than usual. Daphne recovered herself and held Maggie at arm's length. "And thank you, Magpie, for being the most beautiful bride in the whole wide world. Now find Richard and get going."

Holding in her anger at Henry took most of Daphne's energy that week leading up to the weekend in Williamsburg. Intellectually, she knew the anger she was experiencing was at herself. Henry had only said she was drunk because it was true, and just because Richard and Maggie had fallen in love and gotten married didn't mean they were excluding her. She knew all this, yet she couldn't help feeling abandoned and sorry for herself, even enjoying the self-pity in a sort of perverse way. And on top of that, she felt like distancing herself from Henry and hating herself for feeling that way.

On Friday they flew to Richmond together where Tom Flagg had reserved a van for the drive to Williamsburg. He had been looking forward to getting to know Daphne better, but her snippy mood was a definite turn off.

Her mood lifted a bit when she saw the Williamsburg Inn. It's airy, simple elegance was soothing and the thick oriental carpets seemed to muffle her jangling nerves. "Arabella, why don't you share a room with Henry, and I'll take Joe," she said.

"That'll be such fun for me," Arabella replied.

"Our tour guide is going to have dinner with us here, and we'll meet in the lobby at seven, if that's okay with everyone." Daphne looked around at her group.

"I can't join you for any meals until Sunday night, but I'll drive Ludlow over and have him here at seven." Tom Flagg was anxious to leave. Daphne managed to keep her facial expression neutral.

As soon as she and Joe were in the room she went straight to the mini-bar and opened the small bottle of white wine and threw it right back as if it were medicine. She then popped opened the split of Champagne and sipped it while she had her bath. Just before dinner she took half a Valium and felt calm and happy by the time they all met in the hotel lobby. Joe was only seven, after all, and surely wouldn't notice.

Their guide was a slender woman in her 60's with short steel gray hair and a pronounced Virginia accent. She was wearing a dowdy tweed suit, but it looked just right on her. She had a big smile and a lot of enthusiasm for her subject, and everyone took to her right away. Her name was Emma Kyle, and she told them her family had lived in the area since the 18th Century.

At dinner that night Ludlow sat between Emma and Daphne, and while Emma was explaining to the boys some of the finer points of American history, Ludlow turned to Daphne, "By the way, who was that stunning brunette at Maggie's wedding? I had a chance to talk to her at the end, and she's delightful."

"That's Maggie's AA buddy. Della something. I thought she'd bore you.

"Not at all. In fact, she's a fashion writer for a big Chicago news-paper. I thought you'd be interested. She raved about the tent and said all the nicest things about New York, New Yorkers, etc."

"I didn't know she was a fashion writer. Maybe Maggie told me, but I don't think I would have forgotten that. I just thought she was Maggie's minder." Daphne sipped her white wine and turned to Arabella who was sitting on her other side. She did not want to talk about Della.

Arabella said, "I was hoping we'd see more of Tommy this week-end, but I guess it's a working weekend for him with board meetings and so forth. So lucky he could get us these lovely rooms."

"I was hoping to see more of him, too. I like the way he gets things done. Arranging for Emma to be our guide, organizing the van, the hotel, the whole thing."

SLIDING

By Sunday night, Daphne was over her snit, all was amicable with Henry, and she was excited that Tom Flagg was joining them for dinner. Thinking she would be spending time with him, she'd packed some flattering clothes and chose black velvet jeans, a white silk shirt and a tight fitting black vest to wear for dinner. She felt confident that she would be the best looking woman in the hotel dining room. There was definitely no competition in Williamsburg, but her heart was pounding as she applied the final touches to her makeup. *I'd better take a Valium,* she thought, and washed it down with a little white wine.

Chapter 16

"So glad you had such a great honeymoon, but I'm jealous of your tan, Mrs. Blake." Daphne was sitting across from Maggie at Burger Heaven on 51st and Madison.

"How was the weekend in Williamsburg? I can't wait to hear about the mystery man."

"Well, I think I screwed that up. In fact, I probably put him off forever."

"How's that possible? I've never met the man who didn't like you."

"There was an incident. I had an attack of nerves and took just half a Valium before dinner that last night and, mixed with a little wine, it got me very sleepy, and I sort of went to sleep during dinner. To tell the truth, I think I was kind of drunk. I said some not very nice things to Henry at the dinner table before I conked out. I haven't had anything to drink since then. A few Valiums, but no wine."

"Well, it's a start."

"Start? It's not a start. I just had an unfortunate evening. And I'm cutting back. That's all. Don't even *think* you're going to sentence *me* to A.A, Maggie."

"As it turned out for me, even though it *was* an *actual* sentence, it ended up being a reprieve. I can now choose not to drink. Before I had no choice. By eight, I was drinking. Every night."

"Well, I'm not drinking now, and it's no problem for me."

"Just so you know, alcoholism is a progressive disease. It *always* gets worse over time."

"I'm not an alcoholic. I just enjoy drinking. Not drinking is not a problem for me, except Al says I'm no fun."

"I wouldn't worry about Al. Why don't you and the boys come to us for supper on Sunday night? I'll make the Maggie Special. Creamed chicken."

"We'd love it."

Two weeks later Henry and Joe left for Arizona to spend their spring break with Kenny and his parents. Looking forward to being alone for the first time since Thanksgiving, Daphne planned to stay home and watch the classic movie channel. She had declined dinner with Maggie and Richard as well as a black tie dinner at the Varley's with Al to celebrate Chuck's being cleared by the SEC for lack of evidence.

I'll just have a couple of glasses of wine to go with the movies. She thought. *It's Saturday night, after all, and I haven't had anything to drink in weeks.*

Halfway through the second movie and all the way through the second bottle of wine, the phone rang.

"Miss Daphne? This is Fred." It was Ludlow's chauffeur. "I'm with Mr. F. in the emergency room at New York Hospital. I have the car and could come and pick you up, if you want to come."

"Oh, my God. What happened?"

"I think it's a heart attack. They haven't said anything to me yet, but there's a lot of activity in his cubicle."

"Stay there, Fred. I can walk over faster than you can come get me. I'll be right there."

Daphne lowered herself carefully down the stairs and out onto the dark street. As she wobbled eastward toward the nearby hospital, she could feel the panic rising. Was he going to die? Her darling Uncle Ludlow who'd been there for her in crisis and celebration ever since she could remember, how could she ever manage without him?

She'd worked herself up into quite a state by the time she found Fred in the waiting room. Ludlow was being prepped for the operating room, and not being family, it was difficult to get information and impossible to see him. Daphne decided she could handle the situation and took control.

Ludlow's vital signs were still unstable after the six-hour operation. Daphne was frightened, but having kept the vigil with Fred, there was nothing more she could do. The time of waiting and praying had begun.

As the sun was coming up over the East River, Daphne turned the key and let herself back into her house. Chugger and Jazz were waiting for her, full of love.

After feeding them, Daphne plunked herself down at the kitchen table and thought over last night's events. Arriving at the hospital under the influence of two bottles of wine had not endeared her to the triage nurse, and her loud, aggressive behavior had embarrassed Fred. She regretted blabbering on about how important she was to Ludlow and how important Ludlow was to the City of New York. She couldn't believe she'd tried to call the Mayor. She hoped Fred had thought her self-importance came from concern for Ludlow, just a case of nerves. Hours in the waiting room had sobered and subdued her, but the first hour, she was drunk and that arrogance was unstoppable.

Realizing she was at a crossroad, Daphne considered her options. She could call on Maggie or Al. Who would it be? Maggie would drag her to an AA meeting, and Al would fix her a Bloody Mary and expect her to lunch with the Varley's. She looked up and stared at the white plastic phone mounted on the blue and white striped wall in front of her but couldn't decide.

Instead she went upstairs, took three Advil capsules and went to bed. Awaking refreshed at four in the afternoon, she showered, washed her hair and headed back to the hospital. She was not allowed to see Ludlow, and the report was not good. She left Fred there saying she would come back later.

The evening air was cool and soft. It was too early to go home so she went to Al's apartment and found him tuned into the news.

"Daphne, I've been calling you all day and only got the answering service. Where have you been?"

Daphne told him about Ludlow, and they walked over to Mortimer's for dinner. It was one of those clear evenings with the promise of spring in the air, but Daphne was agitated. The Sunday night crowd at the restaurant always included people they knew, and Al thought that would cheer her up, but Daphne couldn't concentrate and wanted to leave after one drink. Al didn't seem to mind and joined some friends at another table. Daphne walked east on 75th Street all the way to York Avenue, then turned right on York for the last couple of blocks. As she came in the door of the hospital, she could see Fred, still there in the bleak waiting room outside the ICU, hunched over, twirling his hat in his hands.

"Any news, Fred?" Daphne could tell from the look on his face that there was no change. "You must be starving. Let's go and get something to eat."

"I think the coffee shop in the hospital's already closed, but there's one on the other side of York Avenue. But not really nice enough for you."

"Of course it's nice enough. Let's go."

Entering the coffee shop, Daphne chose the first booth, near the door. There were only two other customers, both sitting alone in the florescent-lit interior. The waitress came to their table wearing her gray uniform dress and white apron, plasticized menus in hand. She wrote their orders carefully on a small pad with dark blue carbon paper between the leaves. The hamburgers turned out to be surprisingly good. Daphne hadn't realized how hungry she was, and afterwards, reluctant to leave the comfort of each other's company, they ordered coffee.

Drumming her fingers on the table, Daphne tried to ignore the ugly amber glow from the streetlights and the blue neon from the flashing "EAT" sign reflecting on the Formica table. She felt the fear of losing Ludlow in her stomach. It felt hollow even after the burger and fries. Then it seemed to shimmy up and down her spine. She thought of a winter break many years ago. Hanging onto a boyfriend who was speeding crazily on a snowmobile, Daphne knew they were heading for an accident. She remembered feeling relief along with the pain when the collision finally occurred. She was afraid like that now, but she knew there would be nothing but emptiness if Ludlow died.

"What would you do, Fred? I mean, if the worst happened?"

"I'm getting on now, Miss Daphne, but I've got some of money saved up from my years with Mr. F. So, I'd probably be going back to Ireland. I've got nieces and nephews there who wouldn't mind having an old Uncle Fred around to help out. And what about you? I know Mr. F. thinks of you as his own daughter."

"I don't know how I could ever get on without him, Fred. To tell you the truth, my life is a little messed up right now."

"I'm so sorry to hear that, Miss."

"Just can't stand the idea of losing Uncle Ludlow. It seems I need him more now than ever."

"He's going to pull through. You just wait and see. Let me drive you home now. It's late."

"You go on, Fred. I think I'll just sit here for a while. Then I'll walk home. It's only a couple of blocks, and I have an umbrella in my bag."

"Well, if you're sure, then. It's been a long day."

"See you tomorrow. And thanks for everything."

Daphne watched Fred walking over to the car and sipped the last dregs of cold coffee in her cup. The feeling of hopelessness was almost suffocating, imagining a world without Ludlow. All her life, he had been the repository of family memories, replacing a beloved father lost too early in her young life. He was the one always loyal to her father, protecting his memory and in the end protecting her, too. Looking out at York Avenue, now in almost complete darkness, only car lights flashed by.

Okay, God, if you're there, I've got a deal for you. If Ludlow gets well, I'll quit drinking. The thought came to her out of the blue. Was it a prayer or a promise? She didn't know, but suddenly she felt lighter, as though this pact would protect her and dissolve the hopelessness around her.

Daphne was surprised by the strength she felt at that moment, a kind of strength coming from she didn't know where, making her physically stronger, braver, more capable of taking charge of her life. It was a feeling she'd not had in a long time. It reminded her of when she was a young girl, deciding to go out for the tennis team, determined that, whatever was required, she could do it. For the past few years determination had eluded her, but now, though grown up, she knew she was still the same little girl and could call on that sense of resolution. She had it in her.

Ten days later, Fred drove Daphne to LaGuardia to pick up the boys. The plane was due at three. By two-thirty they were already seated in the front row of the gate area, deep in conversation.

"I'll be driving Mr. F. home on Monday. Maybe you'd like to come with us."

"Definitely, Fred. He'll need a lot of help, and you know that'll be hard for him. I'm going to be a mother hen. I know he hates that, but I don't care. I would love you to pick me up everyday at my office around four so I can go out and check on him. Soon we can bring Madame Yamada with us. That'll cheer him up."

"Oh, hello, Daphne!"

Daphne looked up. It was Tom Flagg, briefcase in hand, flight bag slung over his shoulder.

"Tom! Are you coming or going?" Daphne and Fred stood up to greet him.

"Coming." He smiled and held out his hand to Fred.

"This is Fred, Uncle Ludlow's driver. Fred and I have been supervising his recovery at New York Hospital together."

"Nothing serious, I hope." Daphne appreciated the look of concern on Tom's face.

"The crisis is over now, thank God. He's been in the hospital nearly two weeks but goes home on Monday."

Just then the gate opened and Henry and Joe spilled out of the jet-way. "Mom! Mom!" They ran to Daphne, hugging her fiercely. Daphne bent down and kissed the tops of their heads, laughing, fully aware for the first time in a long time of her deep, unshakeable love for them.

"Hi, kids. How're things in Arizona?" Tom asked.

"How did you know we were there?" Joe was amazed.

Tom lifted his eyebrows and cut his eyes toward the gate where the sign was clearly displayed.

"That's cheating!" Henry laughed, remembering Tom was a detective.

"A detective's got to get his information somewhere."

They all walked together to the baggage claim area where Tom left them to go on to the taxi stand.

It had been a long time since Daphne had felt happy. She didn't recognize the symptoms but knew she was sorry to see Tom go.

Daphne had invited Richard and Maggie to join them for an early dinner, and they were waiting at Daphne's house to welcome Henry and Joe home. Richard brought a couple of Frisbees, and he and the boys went straight to the garden. Maggie and Daphne curled up in the library with a cup of tea.

"What a time you've had." Maggie said.

"And I haven't had a glass of wine or a Valium for ten days."

"You're kidding."

"I made a bargain with God, and it looks like he's keeping up his end. So I'm keeping mine – not drinking."

"Oh, Daphne, you can't imagine how happy I am to hear that."

"And you know, I *have* listened to *some* of what you've said, and I admire you, Maggie. I've seen big changes in you, and maybe I'd like to go with you to one of those meetings. Just to see if it's for me or not."

"We can go together tomorrow at lunchtime."

The phone rang. Daphne smoothed her skirt down as she got up to answer it.

A few minutes later Daphne went back to join Maggie on the sofa, tucking her legs under her. "You'll never guess who that was."

"Don't tell me it was the mystery man."

"It was, and he asked me out for dinner next week."

"This *is* good news!"

Outside they could hear the boys laughing and Chugger barking with excitement.

"Listen to those kids." Daphne said. "Come on. Let's go see."

They crossed the living room and stood in front of the French doors, which opened onto a narrow balcony. Richard threw the Frisbee to Henry who dove to catch it. Joe jumped up and down, clapping his hands, waiting for his turn. Chugger circled the garden at full speed, and Jazz, the cat, sat off to the side, close to the kitchen door, washing her face with her paw.

They stood at the doors looking down at the game. Beyond the garden the afternoon sun shimmered against red brick buildings, and the branches of the ginkgo trees were veiled in vivid green.

Daphne cracked the door open an inch and the sharp afternoon chill shafted in. Spring energy palpably vibrated through the room. "Maggie, I'm afraid. I can't do this. I can't stop drinking for the rest of my life."

"What about just not drinking for the rest of today? We'll go to the meeting together tomorrow. Can you do that?"

"Of course. I told you I haven't had anything for ten days."

"Then don't worry about it. Something will happen, and you won't be afraid anymore."

"But I *am* afraid. I feel panicked."

"You can borrow my courage for today."

"What do you mean by that?"

"I mean you can relax and let me worry about anything that needs worrying about."

"But you're *not* worried."

"Exactly. I know everything will be alright, Daphne."

"Okay," Daphne paused. "I'm going to trust you on this, Magpie."

Chapter 17

"Oh my God, Maggie. I'm so glad you answered and not Richard. Tell me it's not too late to call."

"It's midnight, but I'm baking cookies. Don't ask. What's up?"

"I just had the best time ever. That Tommy Flagg can really make me laugh."

"Where'd you go?"

"Pleiades and then Doubles. I made it without even wanting a drink. And Tommy hardly drinks."

"When do I get to meet him?"

"He's in town for the next two weeks. No business trips and we're going out again tomorrow night. And since Uncle Ludlow is getting stronger and stronger, by next week I won't go out to Long Island everyday and will plan a little dinner here. Marie can really cook shad roe. So worth a huge bill from Rosedale's this time of year. How about that on Wednesday night?"

"Count us in. Who else's on the guest list?"

"Just Arabella. Only the five of us. Too bad Uncle Ludlow can't come, but he needs more time to recoup. We'll do it again as soon as he's up and about."

"I've got to take the cookies out of the oven. See you at the office in the a.m."

"I love that we're all in the same office."

"Me, too."

The days of abstinence from alcohol built one upon the other. Daphne found Maggie was right, something did happen, and she was no longer afraid to live a sober life. For such a long time her only choice was to drink. Now that she could choose not to, she felt liberated. The change inside her was so subtle she couldn't explain it or put a date on it, but it was life changing.

Tom Flagg was another story. He traveled often and didn't call her when he was on the road. Daphne dropped hints that she hoped he'd call when he was out of town, but he never did. Tom always seemed to have a good time when he was with Daphne and the shad roe dinner was a great success. Tom had gotten on so well with Maggie and Richard you'd have thought they'd been friends for years, but there was an overhanging presence of secrecy around his job which disturbed Daphne.

In early June, Maggie and Richard came over and stayed on after Henry and Joe had gone to bed. They sat in the big living room with the jukebox turned low, balcony doors open. Daphne asked, "What happens when we go to Maine? Do you think Tom will call or come visit?"

"He's in a highly sensitive business, Daphne. He doesn't call you because it's none of your business where he is or what he's doing or for whom he's doing it. You know that." Richard was bored by constant speculation about Tom Flagg.

Maggie knew Daphne needed to talk and said, "Today's *New York Times* is in the library, Richard. It's Tuesday and you love the science section. Why don't you see what's new?" Relieved to be dismissed, Richard retreated to the library with pleasure.

"Tell me," Maggie said.

"I'm just so frustrated. I know he likes me, and we have so much fun together, but then he leaves town. Sometimes for a week, sometimes ten days, often without warning. Never calls until he gets back. I hate this."

"I don't know him well enough to have any valuable insight, but you can't control his career. Focus on your recovery and enjoy Tom when he can be with you. Richard never called me enough in the early days of our relationship. I remember being very uncertain and disheartened myself for many months."

"You're right, Maggie, and I'm so glad I'm sober, not throwing this away with drunken scenes. A few months ago, I would've really let it rip and that would've been the end of Tom. And as you know, he really respects that I go to AA"

Having Henry and Joe home from school made the days go by quickly and soon it was time for the family to go to Maine. As much as she loved Maine, Daphne didn't like leaving Tom for six weeks and neither did Henry and Joe. Tom had quietly become part of their lives over the past three months, but she hadn't invited him to visit. She knew he'd never have the time. There were just too many business trips.

As planned Maggie and Richard came to Maine for the last week of August and stayed though Labor Day weekend at Daphne's rented cottage on Tennis Club Road.

"Remember last year? The big scene about Al going to the Varley's?" Maggie laughed.

"I'm grateful to be sober. So over all the drama." Daphne sighed.

One afternoon Richard and the boys came back from the village with the mail and blueberry muffins from the Colonel's Bakery. There was a letter from Tom for Daphne. This was totally unprecedented, and she looked up from the envelope in surprise before tearing it open. She read for a few minutes with her open mouth stretching into a dreamy smile as she folded the letter carefully and returned it to the envelope.

They all waited for Daphne to say something. "Let's all go to Jordan Pond for popovers and lemonade this afternoon and save these muffins for tomorrow."

Maggie herded Daphne off by herself, "Well, was that letter from Tom and what did it say?"

"Yes, and it's sort of a love letter. I can't believe it. He told me he's finishing a project, which will take another six to eight months, and then he wants to get a teaching degree. He wants to teach history. Imagine! I'm in love with a prospective teacher after being so rude about the school."

"Sounds very noble but not much of a love letter."

"It says that getting to know me has made him re-think the kind of life he wants to lead, and he doesn't want to be traveling constantly to undiscloseable destinations. I think that's a declaration of some kind, don't you?

"Definitely."

"I'm so crazy about this man."

"I know you are, Daphne, and he's a good one."

"He'll be back in New York next week for a while so how about we all go to the movies or something."

"There's a very sexy movie coming out soon. '*Fatal Attraction.*' We should go and see that."

"And have burgers a P.J. Clarke's afterwards."

"It's a plan."

Ludlow invited Daphne and Tom out to Oyster Bay for Columbus Day weekend in mid-October. The weather was crisp and sunny, and

Ludlow was completely back to his active life. Tom and Ludlow went out early on Saturday morning to play nine holes of golf, and Daphne walked into the village to get the *New York Post*. She took it into the small pine paneled library intending to read, but within minutes she'd dozed off.

Waking up with a jerk, Daphne could hear Tom and Ludlow's voices on the porch discussing something not meant for her ears. The tone of the conversation was confidential. She couldn't really decipher the words, but she could tell this wasn't a casual conversation about the Giants or the Knicks. She tiptoed out into the hall and up the stairs like a thief. While on the stairs, she couldn't help hearing two sentences. This confused and frightened her but, at the same time, made her feel guilty for overhearing.

When they got back to the city on Monday afternoon, Tom dropped Daphne off on 70th Street and promised to come back around seven. The boys had not returned from their weekend with Kenny, and Daphne was alone with the words she'd overheard. She reached for the phone and dialed the Blake's.

"Richard, you won't believe this, but I think Tom is connected with the C.I.A."

"Oh for Pete's sake, Daphne, C.I.A. agents don't have offices in mid-town Manhattan and apartments on the Upper East Side. They're all in Eastern Europe or South America or somewhere."

"No, really. I overheard a conversation between Uncle Ludlow and Tom this weekend, and I'm sure he's involved with something in Mexico. I never know where he goes when he leaves, and he never calls me. And sometimes he leaves in a hurry."

Richard sighed. "There're plenty of things he could be doing in Mexico that aren't part of Central Intelligence. And why would your Uncle Ludlow be involved with anything like that?"

"You're right. But I heard part of a conversation that seemed very strange."

"I think I might know what it is. Ludlow's firm represents Mexican oil interests in the U.S. He was just probably talking about that, and Tom's fluent in Spanish so he may go there on business for the firm."

"I think it must be dangerous, though. Uncle Ludlow said, 'Take every precaution to protect yourself. In Mexico there're ears everywhere.' And that strange letter I got from him this summer said he was going to change his life and become a teacher. I think he is doing something very hush-hush."

"Daphne, if he is, you'd be doing him a disservice discussing it. My advice to you is keep your mouth shut. And Ludlow was probably talking about protecting himself legally."

"Come on, Richard. Find out what you can."

"No. Who knows? It could be dangerous for Tom."

"Never thought of that."

"Your fertile imagination, which I love in jewelry design, is ridiculous in international intrigue, Daphne. But in all seriousness, don't go around talking about this. If I were you I wouldn't bring it up to anyone, not Tom, not Ludlow, not even Maggie or Arabella."

"You're right, but now I'm worried for his safety."

"Then worry with your mouth shut. I'm sure he's just doing some research for Bassel Fowler. Forget about it. And whatever you do, don't you go and become the detective."

Daphne though about it, and it did seem very unlikely that Ludlow would be involved in espionage. Richard was probably right. Just business as usual in the big law firm.

Tom came back for dinner with Daphne and the boys. And after Henry and Joe had gone to bed, they were sitting side by side on the sky blue sofa in the library. Daphne couldn't resist a little detective work. "Wouldn't it be fun to take the boys someplace in Mexico for New Year's?"

"I hate Mexico."

Daphne straightened up, "How can you hate Mexico? Everyone loves Mexico, and you even speak Spanish."

"Oh, I don't really hate Mexico. I just hate the food. Give me Tex-Mex any day."

"Have you been there often?"

"Often enough. How about going to Vermont instead? I'd love to take you and the boys skiing over New Year's."

And so plans were made for skiing in Vermont. Tom rented a chalet on Stratton mountain for a week, and they all piled into Daphne's old station wagon on December 27th and started the two hundred mile drive north after lunch. By the time they left the Taconic Parkway, it was beginning to get dark and small snowflakes dusted the road. The sort of flakes that foretell a storm. Tom was an experienced driver, and there were new snow tires on the car. But as they drove down an incline entering the town of Bennington, Vermont, the car spun out of control and crashed into a parked truck.

Shocked, but otherwise unhurt, Daphne and the boys clambered out of the station wagon. Daphne hugged Henry and Joe to her but hadn't had time to assess the situation before a police car pulled up beside the totaled wagon. Although Tom could speak, it was clear that he needed help. Daphne was grateful for the kindness of the police officer who called the paramedics and drove her and the boys to the hospital right behind the ambulance taking Tom to the ER.

The hospital was clean and efficient and the nurses all wore pristine uniforms and genuine smiles. Quite a nice surprise for the jaded

New Yorkers. Daphne and the boys were checked and pronounced fit, if a bit bruised and shaken. Tom would require surgery to remove his damaged spleen.

Once Tom was settled into a room, Daphne took the boys in a taxi to the Four Chimneys Inn. Not only were their lovely rooms available, but a wonderful innkeeper organized an instructor to take the boys snowshoeing and cross country skiing during the coming week and made all the calls necessary to cancel plans in Stratton. He also took care of what remained of the station wagon. Daphne hesitated before leaving his office, and finally said, "Do you have a list of AA meetings in the area?"

"Certainly," he said and opened the middle draw of his desk and produced a small piece of paper with all the information she needed. There was a meeting that evening at the hospital. Daphne felt comfortable leaving the boys playing Ping-Pong in the rec room with the understanding that they would shower and go to the dining room and order sensible dinners for themselves.

It was still snowing, and Daphne took a taxi back to the hospital where she found Tom sedated and half asleep. Most of the blood work had been done, and surgery was scheduled at seven the next morning. Daphne gave him a kiss and promised to come back to say good night after the AA meeting.

Daphne found the small conference room and slipped into the meeting just as the preamble was being read. Accidentally, she knocked the person sitting next to her with her bag and turned to apologize. An overwhelming sense of peace filled her as she recognized this man as the police officer who drove her to the hospital. Seeing his familiar face beside her reminded her she could trust the process and feel secure that she was being cared for and that everything would be all right. Half way through the meeting she raised her hand, "Hi, I'm Daphne and I'm an alcoholic. I was in a car accident today, and my friend is upstairs awaiting surgery tomorrow morning. My two sons are alone at the Four Chimneys, and I am coping with this without a drink or the desire to drink. Nine months ago I was drunk at a hospital in New York and was so obnoxious to the triage nurse, I'm sure I came close to being thrown out. That night I tried to run the show. Today I am able to ask for the help I need and respond in an adult manner. For me this is a miracle. Thank you all for being here tonight and providing a safe place for me to come and share my experience."

At the end of the meeting a nurse who had been sitting nearby came over to Daphne and gave her a card with a telephone number. "Welcome, Daphne. I'm Helen. Please feel free to call me anytime. I'm working tonight and will look in on your friend. What's the room number?"

"Helen, I'm so grateful. I'm just on my way up there now. Could we go together? I would like to introduce you to Tom."

While the two waited for the elevator, Daphne asked, "Assuming there are no complications, how long is the hospital stay for a healthy young adult having his spleen removed?"

"We'll want him here for a good week and then he should stay nearby for another couple of weeks before he'll be able to travel. But don't worry we have excellent care in this hospital. The best in Vermont."

"It's certainly immaculate, and everyone has been so nice and helpful. I hope to meet the surgeon tonight."

"You will. The surgeons are scrupulous in keeping families and friends informed."

"What a change from the City. I had to fight for every scrap of information in the last situation. And I'm afraid I was arrogant and rude."

"You're a sober woman now, Daphne. Your experiences will be markedly different." They both laughed.

Helen stayed with Daphne while she met the surgeon and said goodnight to Tom. "I came here for the meeting. My shift doesn't start until midnight. So let me run you back to the inn on my way home."

"That would be great. Can you stay and have supper with me?"

"Sorry. I can't. I have two little boys of my own and a husband to see to before I get back to the hospital. I'll be here when you arrive in the morning, though, and will have coffee ready for you."

"That would be so comforting. I feel like I know you all ready."

"We have a special bond."

Back at the inn, Daphne found the boys in the big dining room. They asked about Tom and filled her in on their Ping-Pong match. It had been an exhausting day and soon everyone headed upstairs to their adjoining rooms.

Daphne sat on the edge of her bed, dialed Maggie's number and while listening to the phone ring, looked around the old-fashioned room with pleasure. She could be nowhere else on Earth but New England. The windows were framed with ruffled white organdy curtains, the wallpaper was strewn with blue flower sprigs and the bedspread was made of soft white dotted Swiss. The fire was burning down, but the wood basket was well filled. Suddenly Maggie's familiar voice jolted her back to the present. "Magpie. What a day! Have I got you at a good time?"

"I was opening the door while the phone was ringing. I had a feeling it might be you. How's the house in Stratton?"

"I don't know. I'm at an inn in Bennington. Long story."

Daphne explained all that had happened and asked Maggie to come with Richard to get the boys on January 3rd and take them back to New York. She hoped it wasn't an imposition for them to stay with the boys at her house and oversee homework until she could come back with Tom once he was fit to travel.

"Of course we'd be delighted. What fun to have them all to ourselves!"

"On the drive up, before the accident, I asked Tom about his Mexican connection, and he roared with laughter when I told him I thought he might be a C.I.A. agent. He said what he was doing for Bassel Fowler in Mexico was so mundane he didn't want to tell me as my imagination made him a more exciting character."

"Richard said he probably checks out the people Ludlow's firm are considering representing to make sure they aren't part of some drug cartel."

"Of course. That makes perfect sense."

"I'm so glad you got to a meeting tonight, Daphne, and what good luck one of the nurses was there."

"The most amazing thing about today, Maggie was that I had no feeling of panic. I had no desire to drink but instead had a profound sense that I could handle whatever happened. Last year things would've been totally different. I don't know how this has come about."

"Don't worry about that, Daphne. Your only job is to do what's possible. You can leave the impossible to God."

They said goodnight and Daphne unpacked her things. A small balsam pillow was in the top dresser drawer giving off its sharp, fresh scent. A scent that took her back to her childhood summers in Maine. She picked up the sachet, sank into the fireside chair and inhaled deeply. The peace around her echoed within as Daphne reflected on Maggie's words. She sat motionless with the sachet held to her nose watching the flames turn to embers before crossing to the adjoining room to tuck-in the boys for the night.

About the Author

For nearly two decades, Foster has served on the board of the Hanley Center, an alcoholism and substance abuse treatment center in South Florida. Her mission is to try and remove the stigma surrounding addiction and recovery. By sharing her experience, strength and hope as a board member, speaker and author, she has become an inspirational figure to many inside and outside the recovery community.

Foster's first novel *Below Sea Level* was published in 2013. Set in her native New Orleans, it tells the story of a family torn apart by the disease of alcoholism and how they are healed through hope, forgiveness, and the power of love. *Below Sea Level* won The Illumination Book Award bronze medal for fiction in 2013, also gives practical insight into recovery and the treatment process.

Presaging Foster's foray into novel writing were her studies in English Literature and Art History at Finch College in New York City, where she graduated with honors. Following her studies, she worked at Sotheby's as assistant to the Chairman, John Marion, and later with the famed jeweler, Fred Leighton, before opening her own jewelry design business. Foster is also a passionate horticulturist, and two of her gardens are included in the Smithsonian Archives of American Gardens.

Foster currently divides her time between Florida and France